Ann

RESORT NURSE

RESORT NURSE

ROSE DANA

THORNDIKE
CHIVERS

This Large Print edition is published by Thorndike Press, Waterville, Maine USA and by BBC Audiobooks Ltd, Bath, England.

Thorndike Press is an imprint of Thomson Gale, a part of The Thomson Corporation.

Thorndike is a trademark and used herein under license.

The text of this Large Print edition is unabridged.

Other aspects of the book may vary from the original edition.

Set in 16 pt. Plantin.

LIBRARY OF CONGRESS CATALOGING-IN-PUBLICATION DATA

Dana, Rose, 1912–
  Resort nurse / by Rose Dana.
    p. cm. — (Thorndike Press large print candlelight.)
  ISBN-13: 978-0-7862-9308-7 (alk. paper)
  ISBN-10: 0-7862-9308-X (alk. paper)
  1. Nurses — Fiction. 2. Resorts — Fiction. 3. Large type books. I. Title.
  PR9199.3.R5996R47 2007
  813'.54—dc22   2006035375

BRITISH LIBRARY CATALOGUING-IN-PUBLICATION DATA AVAILABLE

Published in 2007 in the U.S. by arrangement with
Maureen Moran Agency.
Published in 2007 in the U.K. by arrangement with the author.

U.K. Hardcover: 978 1 405 64022 0 (Chivers Large Print)
U.K. Softcover: 978 1 405 64023 7 (Camden Large Print)

Printed in the United States of America on permanent paper
10 9 8 7 6 5 4 3 2 1

To H. William Delong,
diplomat, world traveler and lecturer
unique

CHAPTER ONE

"How would you like to return to Canada for the summer?" the pleasant female voice at the other end of the line asked.

Carol Holly hesitated before replying. Then she said, "I wouldn't mind. It depends on the sort of nursing I'd be doing." The rush to answer the phone in the hall of the quiet Boston rooming house had left her breathless. She had been expecting to hear from the nursing agency through which she worked, and this was the message.

The woman at the agency said, "It's private duty nursing at a resort hotel in a town called St. Andrews, only a few miles from the United States border in New Brunswick."

"I used to live in New Brunswick," Carol said, interested at once.

"I remembered that," the agency woman said. "That's why I kept this job for you."

"St. Andrews is a lovely resort town

overlooking the Bay of Fundy," Carol said. "It should be nice there during the summer months. What sort of case is it?"

"Both difficult and easy," the woman at the other end of the line said. "The patient is a man in his sixties who has just recovered from a stroke and who is a chronic diabetic. He's on his feet but not too well. He's enormously wealthy, used to hold an important post in the State Department, and served on the American consulate staff in Egypt for several years."

Carol's pert face registered interest as she smiled wryly into the receiver. "Sounds like an unusual person."

"He is. The last nurse we sent him lasted only ten days. She found him bad-tempered and not willing to cooperate in taking care of his health. But that was just after he'd gotten out of bed, and he was annoyed at being confined to his apartment. He can go out now, and you would be looking after him in a summer hotel amid surroundings that should improve his disposition."

"When would he want me to begin?" Carol asked.

The woman at the employment agency said, "Right away. He's leaving for the summer resort in a day or two. But he'll have to meet you first and see if you meet with his approval."

"I see," Carol said.

"Don't let that bother you," the agency woman advised. "I have found him very fair. And he'll pay you well for being his nurse and making the trip to Canada and back."

"When should I go to visit him?"

"He wants to see you this evening between seven and seven-thirty," the woman at the nursing agency said. "Will you go?"

"I suppose so," Carol said with a sigh. "If it doesn't turn out, I'll let you know. What is his name and address?"

"He's Arthur Kulas, and he lives at 320 Beacon Street. It's an expensive apartment house, and he has a marvelous place, from what I've been told."

"That's between seven and seven-thirty," Carol repeated again. "I don't want to arrive at the wrong time."

"You have it correctly," the nursing agency woman said brightly. "And I wish you luck."

"From what you've told me, I'm really going to need it," Carol said. Then she thanked the woman and put the phone down.

She walked slowly back along the hall to her room. She was a pleasant girl of twenty-four with jet black hair, cut rather short for the warm weather in a modified boyish

9

style. Her eyes were large and a lovely shade of dark green, and her oval face often lit up with a mischievous smile. A lively sense of humor and good health were among her chief assets, not to mention a smooth olive complexion.

She gave credit for her excellent skin to the Canadian fog of her home city of Saint John. And one of the reasons the call had excited her was because she had grown up only sixty miles from St. Andrews. She'd not spent much time there, since it consisted largely of homes of the wealthy with only a small group of year round local people. Many of the summer tourists who tripled the population rate were guests at the imposing Mic-Mac Lodge and other small hotels and motels. The Mic-Mac Lodge was named in honor of a tribe of Indians who had headquartered in St. Andrews before the advent of the white man.

She remembered her father driving her down there when she was still in high school. They had had dinner together at the smaller Crest Hotel which was located on the principal street, offered good food and boasted a verandah café in warm weather. It had been just the year after her mother's death, and her father had still been trying to give her small treats to take her mind off the tragedy. It had been that year she'd decided to train as a nurse in the big General Hospital in her home city.

In fact, they'd discussed this during dinner that day in St. Andrews. Her father, a precise, graying man of slight build and serious features, had studied her across the table with troubled eyes.

"You're positive you want to be a nurse?" he'd asked.

"Yes."

He hesitated. "You're not doing it because of your mother's death? I mean because you were shocked by it? I'd like to think this is something you decided on your own some time ago."

"I did decide before Mother became ill," she insisted. "I'm not saying that hasn't had some influence on me. But I've always felt that nursing is a wonderful profession for a girl. And I've done well in my home nursing courses."

"So you have," her father agreed with a smile. "And if it's a nurse you want to be, then a nurse you shall be."

And so she'd gone into training as soon as she left school. It hadn't been one grand lark; there had been days, weeks and months of arduous work. At least twice she'd been about to give up and look for an easier

11

profession. And on one occasion she'd flunked an important exam and been in danger of being dropped from her class. Fortunately, she was given the opportunity of writing the paper a second time, and this effort gave her more than a minimum passing mark.

Carol, in student's uniform and cap, now had the exciting experience of taking on important nursing duties. And as she moved into her second and then her third and final year, she'd become a dedicated and competent nurse. Because she'd been encouraged by the nurse in charge of the surgical department, she'd made surgical nursing her speciality.

At the time she graduated, there was a great change in her life. Her father remarried and moved to the larger Canadian city of Montreal. While they were still very close, Carol knew that things would never be quite the same again between herself and her parent. She rented a room and remained in Saint John as a member of the General Hospital nursing staff for another year. And then, being restless and unhappy, she decided to move to the United States. The city of her choice had been Boston, since it was the nearest large city and, with Edinburgh and London, was one of the great centers of medicine.

She had switched from surgical nursing to private duty work. This gave her more freedom, and she was able to move from hospital to hospital as she liked. It also gave her more time to learn about the city and make friends. Making friends had not been that easy, and she still had very few. As for romance, nothing interesting had developed beyond some routine dates with several student doctors who were nearly always too weary to enjoy themselves and in any case had very little money to take a girl out.

As a private duty nurse, she had taken several cases in private homes, but she had tried to avoid these when she could. It meant working under more difficult conditions without any of the benefits a hospital offered her patients. This chance to return to Canada and take care of a patient there for the vacation months would bring her close to her native city for a holiday combined with work. She was glad the woman at the nursing agency had thought of her for the job. She wouldn't be sorry to leave the summer heat of Boston.

She was sitting on the edge of her bed, considering all this, when there was a knock on her door. From outside a friendly young woman's voice said, "It's only me!"

13

"Come in," Carol called to the girl. She recognized the voice as belonging to one of her few friends, Dona Haggerty, another nurse who lived down the hall.

Dona burst into the room. She was a stout blonde girl with a pretty doll-like face and laughing blue eyes.

"I heard you on the phone," she said, coming over to Carol. "Did the agency have anything for you?"

Carol smiled. "They want to send me back to Canada."

"They want to do what?" Incredulous, Dona stood there.

"The case they offered me is a stroke victim who's going to Canada for the summer months. He's going to a resort hotel in St. Andrews, not far from where I grew up."

Dona raised her carefully plucked eyebrows. "Are you taking it?"

Carol got up. "I might. It doesn't sound like too hard a case, and the weather is wonderful down there at this time of year. A lot of wealthy Americans and Canadians go there to be on the bay for the summer."

"Sounds good," Dona admitted. "I only hope you don't change your mind and stay there."

Carol smiled. "Nothing like that. I'd have to return here when my patient does. And

14

anyway, I wouldn't want to remain there after the summer ends, even though I've kept my license renewed to nurse in New Brunswick."

"This house is dead enough," Dona said unhappily. "I wouldn't have a soul to talk to if you left."

"I won't," Carol promised. "I'm just beginning to enjoy Boston."

Dona sighed. "Let's admit, in spite of all the colleges, it's not the fun spot of the world for a single girl. But there are worse places. We do have a lot of entertainment available. And who knows? Maybe by fall the supply of men will be more interesting."

Carol laughed and put her arm around her friend. "See that you work on your diet and exercise before I get back. I'll expect you really to have slimmed down."

The stout blonde pouted sadly. "Do you think it's because I'm a fat girl I have hardly any dates?"

"Could be!"

"You don't do much better," Dona pointed out.

"I don't have your charm," Carol said. "You'd be a sensation, with your face and blonde hair, if only you were thinner."

"You're making me feel like one of those girls in the before and after advertisements

15

for reducing pills," Dona said forlornly. "But I'll try. I'll surprise you when you get back."

"I'll count on that," Carol said. "If we're to make a team of *femme fatales* you have to do your part."

"When will you be leaving?" the stout girl wanted to know.

"I'm not sure about that yet," Carol admitted, moving over to the bureau and finding the scrap of paper on which she'd written the name and address of her prospective patient. She turned to Dona again. "The man is very wealthy and hard to please. His name is Arthur Kulas, and he lives in an apartment at 320 Beacon Street."

Dona showed surprise. "The lecture man!"

Carol asked, "You've heard about him?"

"If it's the same man," her friend said. "The one I mean is striking-looking and around sixty. He used to be in the diplomatic service, and his hobby now that he's retired is giving lectures on the Middle East. He did his 'Caravans and Costumes' show for our hospital alumnae about a year ago. It was excellent."

Carol smiled. "It sounds like him."

"But you say he's paralyzed. The man I heard lecture was very active and healthy-looking."

16

"He's only had a slight stroke," Carol said. "And he has apparently recovered from it now. But he has diabetes to complicate matters, and his doctor feels he needs someone to keep an eye on him. Since he's a wealthy man, it's a luxury he can afford."

"It must be the same one," Dona decided. "I heard some of the girls saying he came from a famous Boston family, even though he has a foreign-sounding name. I guess the connection was on his mother's side. Anyhow, he knows all there is to know about art in the Middle East. He wore a lot of authentic costumes and showed us some ancient wall hangings, Persian rugs, hammered copper and elegant brocades. And he put it all together in a show of music and action that made it live."

"He sounds like fun," Carol said. "But I hear he's been having some trouble keeping nurses."

"I don't doubt he's an individualist," her friend agreed. "And they are always hard to work for. But he has charm, if it's the same Arthur Kulas. If he were twenty years younger, I'd be trying to steal the job from you."

"You might still have the chance." Carol laughed. "He may not like me at all. I'm seeing him tonight a little after seven."

It was exactly two minutes past seven when she found herself in front of the imposing red brick apartment house at 320 Beacon Street. It had white trim at doors and windows, thick Georgian pillars at the front entrance and white shutters at the windows, giving it a traditional New England appearance despite its size. For some reason Carol was oddly nervous. She'd never felt this way before when meeting a prospective patient. Probably it was because she'd heard so much about Arthur Kulas and knew he'd be difficult to communicate with. Or at least that was the impression she'd received.

Also, the job meant a good deal to her. She was suddenly looking forward to seeing her native country again, and this assignment could provide her with an excellent chance. With a sigh she decided to assault the dragon in his tower and mounted the several granite steps to the entrance.

She had dressed carefully for the occasion in a two piece outfit of gray orlon and wool. The dress had a pleated mini-skirt, and the jacket buttoned on the right and had a high collar of silver braiding. To match it she wore a silver tam and carried a small silver bag. It was stylish and yet sober enough to suggest her professional occupation as a nurse.

Apparently she met the approval of the elderly uniformed doorman. He at once phoned the apartment of Arthur Kulas. When he finished the brief conversation, he smiled at her and escorted her to a self-service elevator.

"It's the top floor, Miss Holly," he said. "Mr. Kulas is expecting you. Apartment 52."

She thanked him, stepped into the stainless steel elevator with its chrome buttons and pressed the right one.

When she got out at the proper floor, she was struck by the great luxury of the apartment building. The corridor was wide, and its walls were freshly painted in a soft beige, while the matching rug's thick pile gave her the feeling of richness.

At the end of the corridor a door was open, and standing silhouetted against the bright light of an inner hall was a slim, distinguished-looking man.

Carol had a sinking feeling as she approached the figure staring at her silently. As she came close to the doorway, she was able to study her prospective patient. Her first surprised reaction was that he looked anything but ill. He was thin and alert. And

19

though his fine matinee idol's features were slightly eroded by age, he was still a handsome man and could easily be taken for forty. His hair was blond flecked with gray, and his eyes were a penetrating blue. He wore a London style gray tweed suit and a red and white checked shirt, together with a dark crimson tie and a matching handkerchief in his jacket pocket.

"You are Miss Holly, of course," he said in a pleasant actor's voice as he extended his hand to her. "I'm Arthur Kulas."

"How do you do, Mr. Kulas?" she said, accepting his hand. His grip was firm and not like that of an invalid.

"I don't do well or I shouldn't be requiring the services of a nurse," he said with the suggestion of a twinkle in his blue eyes. "Come in and let me show you my place."

"It's a lovely apartment," she said, studying the white walls of the hall with marbleized posts dividing it at intervals. The hall was a veritable art gallery, with a large display of paintings along its entire length. Even the runner was of a beige, brown and sand geometric pattern that complemented the art display.

Arthur Kulas went ahead to guide her. "I spent six months redoing this place," he said. "I blasted out walls to bring a special power line up here to light this entrance hall gallery. You'll see I have works by Jean Dufy, Bruno Caruso, Mario Coppala and Pierre Bonnard among others."

Carol was left speechless by the finest collection of paintings she'd ever seen in a private home. There were oils, watercolors and drawings all in suitable frames. They ranged from impressionist to abstract and from European landscapes to dark New England portraits of another era.

At last she turned to him with a delighted smile. "How wonderful to be able to assemble a collection like this for your very own."

The distinguished gray-haired man looked pleased. "I've enjoyed it. And it's given me something to do since my retirement. Everything else in the place is an anticlimax after the gallery, so we'll just sit down in the living room and get to know each other."

The drawing room with its white marble fireplace, antique French needlepoint rug and great velvet sofas was no anticlimax as far as Carol was concerned. It was perfect and suited her host.

He was standing at a sideboard. Looking over his shoulder, he said, "I do hope you enjoy wine. It seems right we should begin our discussion over some good sherry."

"Wine is the only alcoholic drink I do like," Carol said. "I'd be glad to have a sherry with you."

Arthur Kulas sighed with relief as he poured their drinks from an antique colored glass decanter. He came over and handed her a glass of the amber liquid. "My last nurse had an unfortunate addiction to ginger ale. It was one of her more distressing aspects." He sat primly on a sofa at right angles with the one on which Carol nervously sat. He lifted his wine glass. "To Canada and a pleasant summer."

Carol sipped her wine and relaxed just a little. "You seem so well," she said.

"I am very well at the moment, but my stubborn doctor insists that I require a watchdog to keep me that way. I'm not allowed to smoke or eat all the things I like. He says he's trying to prevent a big stroke."

"That's a very good plan," she agreed.

Arthur Kulas showed mild annoyance. "But when you've reached my age, you feel you should be able to live as you like."

Carol smiled. "Yet I don't imagine you enjoyed life much when you were in the hospital. Isn't it wiser to be moderate and remain well?"

He eyed her apprehensively. "I hope you're not given to making touching philosophic speeches like that. I couldn't bear it."

She was forced to laugh at his dismay. "I don't think I am really. I'm a little uneasy on meeting you."

"It's I who should worry," he protested. "If I take you on as my nurse, you'll be the warden and I the prisoner."

"I'd try not to make the relationship obvious," she promised, sipping some more of the excellent wine.

"I use insulin by hypodermic, of course," Arthur Kulas said. "And you would be responsible for giving me my injections."

"I've had several diabetic patients," she said.

"I have to take it three times a day," the distinguished-looking man said. "What do you know about the sixteen-day plan?" He shot the question at her quickly as if he wanted to catch her off guard.

He almost did. But she soon remembered her training. "You're referring to the forty-eight sites of injection. Using them, you allow sixteen days between injections at the same site and so avoid making the skin less elastic and delaying absorption of the insulin."

The man on the velvet sofa gave an approving nod. "That's the correct answer.

My doctor hopes I will soon be able to limit myself to one or two injections a day, and that would make the problem less complex. I'm also taking medicine to thin my blood, and from time to time my blood samples must be carefully measured for clotting."

"I know the procedures," Carol assured him.

Arthur Kulas seemed impressed. "I'm glad to hear that," he said. "And I understand you are a Canadian by birth; that you come from New Brunswick, in fact."

"Yes. I lived there most of my life."

He eyed her shrewdly. "Your enthusiasm for this post is not because of a desire for a free trip home to Canada, is it?"

She blushed. "No. Of course I will enjoy being in St. Andrews for the summer if you should hire me. It's a lovely area."

"I know all about it," the wealthy man said. "I've been there many summers. It happens I'm a shareholder in the Mic-Mac Lodge, a rather large shareholder. Since my retirement, I've gone down there every year."

"Then you're well acquainted with it."

"Obviously," he said. "There is one other important point I have to bring up, regardless of how awkward it may be for both of us."

Carol held her breath. "Yes?"

The slim man put his empty wine glass down on the ornate coffee table before him. "I trust you're not a romantic type, Miss Holly."

Again she felt her cheeks warm. "I'm not sure what you mean."

"Some young women enter the nursing profession in the hope of marrying a wealthy doctor or patient. I hope you are not one of those most insufferable females, for I've already gone through one trial with an attractive young nurse about your own age. I am not considering marriage now or in the future. I'd like to make that plain."

"Of course," she said. "And if that's what you mean by romantic, then I'm not romantic."

He studied her suspiciously. "You seem such a paragon, I should probably not hire you on general principles."

Carol didn't know whether to be angered or amused. Arthur Kulas was living up to his reputation of being difficult. She put down her empty glass and said, "That's up to you. I probably have plenty of minor vices that I'm concealing from you."

The wealthy man looked interested. "Really? Such as what?"

"I like all the time I can manage to myself," she said. "I never allow myself to become involved with a patient's ailments. Too hard on me."

He didn't look shocked. "That seems eminently sensible."

"I like to play tennis when I can and go to late parties if any are available," she went on. "And I'd insist on having top accommodations on a level with your own and complete social freedom." She tossed this last in on an inspiration. She decided the only way to cope with Arthur Kulas was to speak his language.

The wealthy man looked pleased. "I agree," he said. "I'll hire you."

She wasn't going to fall dead with gratitude. That would be a sure way to make him change his mind. So she ignored his acceptance of her and gave her attention to a golden figurine on one of the sideboards.

"What a lovely figure," she said, indicating it.

He nodded. "Came out of a tomb along the Nile. Worth a penny! Perhaps I should tell you there's an element of risk in working for me."

"Oh?" She stared at him.

"Yes. This apartment has been broken into three times recently. My belongings have been ransacked and several items stolen from me. Luckily, they left the figure you admire. But once when they caught me at home, I was struck on the head. It wasn't serious, but another time it might be. As my companion, you'll share the same risk."

CHAPTER TWO

Carol was startled by the warning and the calm way in which the slim, gray-haired man offered it. She knew that he must have a small fortune in items of art in the apartment, but the idea of thieves hadn't entered her head until he mentioned it.

She asked, "Is this a recent development?"

"Fairly recent," he said. "The thefts were made after I recovered from my stroke and after I'd moved to this apartment. There were several newspaper articles about the improvements I'd made here, and they mentioned my collection of Middle East antiques and the art gallery."

"You think those stories brought you to the thieves' attention?"

"I expect so," Arthur Kulas said with a bleak expression on his classic face. "Of course I gave a large number of lectures on the art of the Middle East before I became ill. That also gave me exposure, especially since I use priceless examples of silks and brocades, not to mention fine rugs, in the presentation."

She said, "Well, surely you'd be safe away from here. In St. Andrews, there would be no point in thieves bothering you."

"On the contrary," the wealthy man said. "I'll be taking along my lecture material. I propose to begin doing the shows again now that I'm feeling better. And I've already promised the manager at the Mic-Mac Lodge to begin there."

"I see," she said. "Does the doctor think you should?"

"As soon as I am able to cut down to two insulin injections a day," he said. "And I hope that may be within a week." He paused. "Well, I've placed all the facts on the table, Miss Holly. Are you still willing to accompany me to St. Andrews?"

She smiled. "Yes, I think so."

"Fine," he said in a businesslike way. "Do you drive?"

"Yes," she said. "I have a license but no car."

"We won't worry about a car," Arthur Kulas said. "I have a large station wagon. It will be loaded with my things, and we can share the driving. I'm afraid you'll have to do most of it. But I'm positive we can make it to St. Andrews in a single day."

"With the expressways extending most of the way, I can't see why we shouldn't," Carol agreed.

"Can you be ready to leave the day after tomorrow?"

"I think so."

"Excellent," he said. "Be here with your luggage no later than eight in the morning. I'll have a man from the garage help us pack the car. The heavy items will be the trunks with the materials for my lecture. When we arrive at the hotel, there will be no problem getting unloaded."

Carol stood up. "I'll be here at eight sharp," she said. "If there is any delay or change of plans let me know through the agency."

"I'll do that," he agreed, rising. "But there isn't likely to be a delay. I'm anxious to get away from the city."

He escorted her to the door. She received the impression that he wasn't really the ogre he pretended to be. In spite of his directness, he was really a rather considerate person.

She smiled to herself as she left the apartment house for the short walk home. Pausing briefly to wait for a traffic light to change, she was surprised to have a hand touch her arm and a male voice say, "Just a

29

minute, miss."

She turned to stare into the square, tanned face of a young man about her own age. He was wearing a brown Nehru jacket and a turtle-neck sweater of a lighter brown material.

Not recognizing him, she said coldly, "Yes?"

Holding up a small change purse, he said, "I believe you lost this."

Carol frowned and held up her silver pocketbook. "You're wrong. This is the only purse I'm carrying."

The young man showed astonishment. "Are you sure?"

"Positive?" she said. Glancing at the light, she saw that it had changed. Now she had to wait until it flashed green again before she could move. She carefully turned her back on the stranger.

"I'm terribly sorry," he said, still standing there.

"It's all right," she said curtly without looking his way.

"The trouble is I picked the wrong girl," he said with concern.

She glanced at him with a frown, deciding that perhaps she would report him to the first policeman she saw. He could be some kind of lunatic. But a glimpse of his worried face was reassuring. He looked like an honestly distressed young man.

"There were two of you passing along the sidewalk at the same time. I knew one of you must have dropped this. You were going in opposite directions. I picked you, and it took me a few minutes to catch up with you." He glanced back disconsolately. "I've lost her for good."

"You can put a notice in the paper," Carol suggested, "under 'Lost and Found.' "

"I'll do that," he said, studying the small brown purse with a furrowed brow. "I'm sorry I ever saw this. Just finding it gives me a responsibility."

She smiled. "I wish you luck." And noting the light had changed, she left him to start across the street.

But she hadn't left him behind after all. He was striding along at her side. "I'm sorry I held you up," he said. "If you don't mind, I'll walk along with you. The newspaper office is down this way. I wonder if they take classifieds in the evening?"

"I'm sure I don't know," she said, stifling any warmth in her voice. He was probably a perfectly respectable young man, but it didn't do to take chances.

The dark-haired young man must have sensed her reaction to him. "I hope you don't think I'm some sort of crazy person," he said.

"I'm not in the habit of making friends with strangers," she said, looking straight ahead as she strode quickly along. They were passing the big park known as Boston Common, and she stared hopefully for a sign of a policeman. Of course there was none in sight.

"I realize that," the young man said, easily keeping up with her frantic pace. "But I did find the purse. I didn't just make it up as an excuse to speak to you. I don't make a habit of picking up girls I don't know, either." There was an injured note in his voice.

Carol had suddenly come to a crossing where there was another traffic light against her and too many cars passing for her to dare walk against the light. She took the opportunity to give the young man a reproving look.

"I don't want to be hateful," she said. "And you're probably a nice person. But I don't know you, and it isn't fair of you to push your company on me this way. I may hail somebody and ask him to help me get rid of you."

His tanned young face showed dismay. "You wouldn't do that?"

"If you persist," she warned him.

"But I only want to be friendly," he said.

She met his eyes with a firm glint in her own. "I don't know you."

"I'll introduce myself," he said, quickly taking a bulging wallet from his pocket. He opened it to a driver's license. "Walter Pitt," he said. "I'm a writer. At least I'm trying to be. I graduated from Harvard last year. You can find out everything about me on these identification cards." He offered her the opened wallet.

She pushed the wallet away. "It's all right. I don't want to discuss it."

"Now you're being unreasonable and Victorian," he accused her. "Here we live in a swinging age, and you're acting this way!"

"I wish you'd oblige me by swinging in some other direction," she said. The light changed, and she started walking again, head high, a hint of anger marring her pretty face.

The young man was still at her side. "I'm not bothering you," he said. "I'm only talking and trying to be friendly. I really did think it was your purse."

He sounded so completely let down she was forced to smile. She said, "If you're really going to the newspaper office, we'll be parting at the next corner. I go in the other direction."

"Then we'll be parting," he said. "I have to put that notice in the Lost and Found column."

She felt relief at this announcement. "I'm glad to hear you're not a fake."

"Do I look like a fake?" he asked in despair. "You're giving me a complex, making me think I go around looking like some kind of criminal. Is it my face?"

Carol laughed. "No. There's nothing wrong with your face. It's just that the circumstances of our meeting made me suspicious."

"I couldn't help finding the purse," he argued.

"I'm not saying you could. And it's all right. So we'll part friends." They had come to the corner.

The tanned young man smiled. "I'd like us to do that," he agreed. "You know my name is Walter Pitt, but I don't know yours."

She hesitated. Deciding it could do no harm to tell him, she said, "It's Carol Holly."

"And you're a schoolteacher," he said triumphantly. "I can tell."

It was her turn to be upset. "What could possibly make you think that?"

He waved airily. "It's written all over you.

You're so prim and correct. You have a classroom manner."

She looked at his smiling face indignantly. "How can you manage to be so dogmatic? Lots of schoolteachers are what you call swingers."

"Granted. But you're not one of them."

"I don't even happen to be a school-teacher," she fumed.

"Sorry," he said. He considered, his hand on his chin. "I've got it," he said, his face brightening. "You're a librarian. You've got that silence-in-the-reading-room look about you."

Carol was growing more and more upset. "It happens you're wrong again! I'm a nurse."

He stared at her in innocent surprise. "I'd never have dreamed it," he said. "I mean, all the nurses I've ever met have been so sophisticated."

"Really?" she said with sarcasm. "Well, they probably haven't had madmen stopping them in the street and asking a lot of questions." And she turned and started off home.

The sound of dogged footsteps continued, and although she didn't look to right or left she knew he was following her again. Carol accelerated her pace.

35

"I'm not following you," the young man said breathlessly.

"You're giving a reasonably good imitation, then," she told him, short of breath herself now.

"I just wanted to say I'm sorry, and could I call you some time?" he pleaded.

"I don't care whether you're sorry or not, and you can't call me because I'm leaving Boston. That is very lucky for me, considering the streets are being overrun with lunatics like you."

"I've proven I'm not a lunatic, and I'm sorry you thought I insulted you," the young man at her side went on. "And you're making me practically run blocks out of my way."

"Run in the opposite direction any time you like," she said angrily. "I'm just looking for a policeman."

"All right; you win," he said unhappily. "But the next time we meet, you're going to feel awfully foolish about this."

"The next time we meet will be never!" she snapped. But she snapped to empty air, for the young man had fallen behind and left her.

No sooner had she reached her room than Dona came in to find out if she'd gotten the job. "Are you going to Canada?"

Carol smiled. "Day after tomorrow. We're driving."

"Lucky you!" her friend exclaimed. "And it was the Arthur Kulas I spoke of, wasn't it?"

"It was. He's eccentric but rather pleasant. To be truthful, I'd almost forgotten about him. I had a weird experience just outside his apartment." And she went on to tell of her meeting with the young man.

Dona listened with rapt attention. "I wish I had your luck! If I met anyone as nice as that, I wouldn't insult him and run away from him."

Her friend's comment only served to make Carol feel guilty. She had been terribly abrupt with Walter Pitt, as he'd called himself. But she defended her behavior saying, "He did what amounted to trying to pick me up on the street. I think you'd have reacted in the same way."

But Dona was lost in dreamy reflection. "He sounds romantic to me. And he's a writer as well."

"Trying to be one," Carol said. "There's a lot of difference."

Dona smiled. "Next time you find something like that, bring it home to me."

"And I'm sure you wouldn't thank me." Carol laughed, as they dismissed the matter

37

of the young man to discuss her new job.

Two days later, Carol drove her patient's station wagon along the Maine Turnpike at the seventy-mile speed limit. It was a beautiful morning in late June. Traffic wasn't too heavy, and Arthur Kulas sat beside her in an apparently relaxed mood now that the flurry of packing and getting on the road was over.

Her patient had given Carol the good news that he would only be required to take two insulin shots a day unless the daily tests she made of his condition suggested the sugar content in his blood was rising. The scenery along the turnpike was not as spectacular as the coastal road would have been, but they saved a lot of time by taking the fast expressway. And with Carol's employer still in a precarious state of health, it was the better route for them.

Rolling green fields of dairy farms and evergreen forests lined the route. Once in a while, when they passed close to a town, they would catch a glimpse of housing developments with rows of drab little houses set out in too precise patterns.

After they'd been on the road awhile, Carol asked, "Are you feeling all right?"

The distinguished-looking man on the seat beside her regarded her peevishly.

"That is a question I'd prefer you not ask me. I don't intend to spend so much time worrying about my health that I haven't any left to enjoy it." And he turned away from her to stare out at the passing fields.

To change the subject, Carol asked, "How did you happen to start your series of lectures?"

The retired diplomat smiled. "It began in a very ordinary way," he told her. "First I entertained my friends at the apartment. I had a very nice place in Cambridge before I moved to Beacon Hill. They were so ecstatic about the marvelous fabrics, rugs and art pieces I showed them they suggested I do some charity performances. From that point on it became a professional undertaking with me."

"I have a friend who saw one of your performances," she told him. "And she felt the best part of the show was your fund of stories about the Middle East."

He nodded appreciatively. "I had a number of exciting experiences when I was there. It's a hive of espionage, black market deals, and teeming with all kinds of exotic characters. You should visit there one day."

"I'd like to," she said, her eyes on the highway ahead.

"One of my most interesting assignments

as a member of the consulate staff came shortly before I retired from the service," Arthur Kulas told her. "I was sent as observer with a party of archeologists exploring the tomb of Khenetma. They made some fabulous finds, discovering a hidden cache of jewelry that was priceless. I became very friendly with a man called Sousa who was contractor for the workmen doing the actual excavating. A likable fellow of Lebanese origin. But it turned out he was a scoundrel."

"In what way?" she asked.

"He stole a great deal of the treasure for himself," Arthur Kulas told her. "He had the workmen secretly remove some of the jewelry from the tomb before the archeologists had made an inventory of it. Of course they discovered the stuff was being taken in the end, but not before Sousa had gathered a fortune in precious stones and gold and hidden it away in a secret cache. I found it hard to believe such a friendly chap could be guilty of a crime like that. The expedition was paying him well."

"I suppose the temptation was just too great."

"Apparently. That's the difficulty in making sudden friendships with people. Unless you know them fairly well, you simply can't

40

trust them, because you don't know what degree of dishonesty to expect. Sousa wound up with a long prison term, of course. The Egyptian government does not like its national treasures plundered. In the old days they would have cut off both his hands."

Carol shuddered. "That seems overly drastic."

"Drastic but effective," her patient said calmly. "A rather touching thing happened after Sousa was imprisoned. His cousin came to the consulate and presented me with three very fine hand-woven rugs of unusual design. He said they had been woven by Sousa's wife and daughter, and the unfortunate fellow had given him explicit instructions to make a present of them to me in remembrance of our friendship."

"Quite a tribute," she said.

"I thought so," Arthur Kulas agreed. "They were such fine specimens I use them in my show. They are very colorful. You'll see them. I have brought them along. It was not long after I was given the rugs that I came down with severe hepatitis. They sent me back to Washington and, when I recovered, offered me the choice of minor duties, because of my health, or retirement."

"And you chose retirement?"

41

"Yes. Minor duties would have meant nothing in a career sense. I'm a wealthy man, and with my health in a dubious state it seemed stupid of me to go on. It's worked out very well. My lecture work has become more important each year. If it weren't for this miserable diabetes and the stroke that followed it, I'd be busy and happy today."

"You must be improving," she said. "The doctor has cut down on your insulin."

"I suppose so," he said gloomily. "This plague of robberies, on top of everything else, has been almost too much."

"Perhaps they are over as well," she said.

He gave her a sharp glance. "Miss Holly," he said in his acid tone, "another thing I find nauseating is excessive optimism."

"Sorry." She smiled at him. "I think you're getting tired. And we soon should have something to eat. We can stop in Bangor before driving to the border."

"I'm perfectly all right," her patient insisted petulantly. But his rather handsome face looked more worn and weary than she had ever seen it. She made no further comments but decided they would stop to have food in Bangor whether he wanted to or not. She knew how dangerous it was for a diabetic not to have nourishment to cover his insulin intake.

The restaurant she chose in the Maine city was modest but seemed to have good food. Arthur Kulas was not impressed by it. He complained about their table, and after they'd been moved nearer a window he fussed that the only view they had was of a used car lot. And he sat frowning at the menu for long minutes before finally making a choice. He decided on scallops and gave minute instructions on how they were to be prepared. Carol chose the dinner for the day, which was beef stew, and hoped things would go well.

But they didn't. When the scallops arrived, Kulas sat looking at them with undisguised disgust. He glared at Carol and said, "If fools don't control the world, it's not because they aren't in the majority! How could anyone but a moron prepare a dish like this?"

Carol sighed. "My stew is good. Why not have them bring you some?"

He sat up very straight. "I have an aversion to stew."

"You must eat something," she worried.

At last he began picking at the scallops but ate only a few of them. As a result of his lack of nourishment, for the rest of the drive over the narrow country road that was a short cut to the Canadian border, he sat listless and silent.

By the time they'd stopped at the border for immigration and customs examination, Arthur Kulas was looking really ill. Carol had consulted the map and knew that St. Andrews was only about eighteen miles away. She hoped that he would be all right until they reached the resort hotel.

She glanced at him when they'd covered about half the short journey and became thoroughly alarmed. Arthur Kulas was slumped in his seat with glazed eyes and seemed to be trembling. Recognizing the symptoms, she knew he was sinking into hypoglycemic shock.

CHAPTER THREE

Because she was driving beyond the speed limit, Carol reached the center of the town within a few minutes and at once turned the car into the first gas station for information.

As she rolled down the window, a youth came out to serve her. She said, "I'm looking for the hospital. I have a very sick man here. Is there one in St. Andrews?"

The boy nodded. "A small one. It's two blocks over and three blocks up. You can't miss it. There's a sign outside, and its a big white house. But I don't know if Dr. Shaw is there or not."

"Is there just one doctor?"

"Yep," the youth said. "Dr. Bill Shaw is the only one here now since Dr. Merril died last year. But there are a couple of nurses at the hospital."

"Thanks," she said hastily, not wanting to waste any more time. Since Arthur Kulas remained slumped silently on the seat, she was certain now he was in coma. Accelerating the station wagon out into the street again with such frenzied speed the wheels squealed in rebuke, she drove down the two blocks the youth indicated and then turned left.

It was an uphill drive, since the town was situated on a hillside extending down to the ocean on which the main street fronted. The streets were unusually wide, and there were fine old houses with plenty of majestic elms to give shade. It looked like any dignified New England town, and yet she was back on Canadian soil again.

She hesitated at the intersection and looked anxiously for the hospital sign as she came to the third block. And there on the right was the sign, in gold letters on a black background. There was a gravel driveway leading to the entrance of the small hospital, and she headed the car toward it.

Reaching the front door, she turned off the engine and hurried out of the car to summon help for her desperately ill patient. She rang the bell impatiently, and after what seemed an endless time a short, fleshy woman in the white uniform and cap of a nurse opened the door with an air of mild annoyance.

"Yes?" she said.

"I have a man in the car who's terribly ill," Carol told her. "It's diabetic coma. Is the doctor in?"

The nurse looked less annoyed. "He's in his office. I'll get him." And she hurried off, leaving the door open.

Carol went back to the station wagon and, opening the door, tried to rouse the sick man. But it was no use. She was still there when the nurse came out, followed by a tall, serious young man in a dark business suit.

"What's the problem?" he asked.

"My patient is in diabetic coma," Carol explained. "He missed his lunch on the way here."

"You're his private nurse?" the young doctor said, bending forward to examine the unfortunate Arthur Kulas.

"Yes."

Dr. Bill Shaw was already lifting the limp

figure out of the station wagon and expertly balancing him over his shoulder to carry him into the hospital. Carol and the older nurse followed as the doctor took Arthur Kulas into his treatment room and placed him on a sofa.

The young doctor hurried to his medicine cabinet, took out a hypo and found a vial with which he filled it. As he went over to the still unconscious man, he said, "Adrenalin. This should do it."

Carol stood by nervously as the doctor administered the hypo. Then he remained by the bed to watch the reaction. The patient's eyelids fluttered, and he stared up at them dazedly. The color was returning to his face, and his recovery appeared to be rapid.

After a moment, he asked, "What happened?"

Dr. Bill Shaw stared down at him. "You allowed yourself to go without food too long. You mustn't do that again."

"Food!" Arthur Kulas sat up in disgust. "You call what they offered me in Bangor food?"

"I don't know what the problem was," the young doctor said with a reproving glance for Carol. "But your nurse should have seen to it you ate."

Carol blushed furiously. "I did try to make him eat. He didn't seem to realize the danger."

"It wasn't her fault," the wealthy man on the sofa said. "I'm solely to blame." He frowned and glanced around him. "Where am I?"

"At the hospital in St. Andrews," Bill Shaw replied. "Your nurse showed good judgment in getting you here without delay."

"I have every confidence in Miss Holly," Arthur Kulas said testily. He glared at the doctor. "Who are you?"

"Dr. William Shaw," the young man said. "May I ask your name?"

"You may. It's Kulas," the wealthy art collector said, still in a bad humor. "My doctor was supposed to write to you about my coming here for the summer. He wanted you to keep an eye on me."

The young man's face brightened. "Kulas? Of course. I got the letter a few days ago. We're happy to have you here in St. Andrews again, sir."

The man on the sofa looked glum. "In all the years I've been here, I have never had to see a doctor. I didn't even know the town had a hospital. But I've had a stroke in the past year. I'm an old crock now."

The doctor smiled. "I wouldn't take that

attitude. Many people have made fine recoveries from strokes." He looked at Carol again. "I'm in contact with his local doctor, and you can come to me any time you require help. I'll be checking him regularly on his regular physician's instructions."

From the sofa, Arthur Kulas said, "It sounds very much as if you expect to have a busy summer simply treating me. I warn you I do not like too much attention."

"I won't have time to give you much once the regular rush of summer visitors arrives here," Dr. Bill Shaw said. He was a broad-shouldered young man with a serious face, not really handsome but good-looking. His hair was sandy, and he had a few freckles.

Arthur Kulas rose to his feet shakily. "Thank you, Dr. Shaw," he said. "I expect I'll get a bill for your services."

"Indeed you will." The young man smiled. "I'll stop by the hotel and see you after dinner. I suggest you have room service bring up your food. And I'll bill you for the evening call as well."

The eccentric art collector glared at him, then turned his attention to Carol. "I'm well enough to check in at the hotel now. I think we should be on our way."

"You're sure you feel strong enough?"

The classic face of the wealthy man had

regained its assurance. "Miss Holly," he said severely, "if I'm going to be required to say everything twice for your benefit, we're not going to get on well at all." And he started for the door on his own.

Dr. Bill Shaw offered Carol an understanding smile. "I'll see you when I call on the patient tonight," he said.

"Yes," she said somewhat shyly. And she hurried out to see her patient safely in the car.

The drive from the hospital to the Mic-Mac Lodge was a short one. The big hotel was located on a hilltop overlooking the town and the Bay of Fundy. It was a large building and had been constructed in English Tudor style. Except for its massive size, it resembled a country inn.

"It's a half-century old," her patient said as they drove up to the steps leading to the broad verandah and lobby of the hotel. "In those days they built for comfort, so we'll have decent-sized rooms."

Carol liked the looks of everything she saw, from the rambling four-story main building to the lavish gardens with their flower beds. There were shuffle boards, putting greens, an enormous kidney-sized swimming pool, and across the lawn a building which Arthur Kulas referred to as the Casino.

"It's where they have dancing, movies and bingo," Arthur Kulas said as Carol assisted him out of the station wagon. He was still shaky on his feet.

Carol nodded. "And I see they have at least three tennis courts beside it."

"You do play tennis, don't you?" he asked.

"I have my racquet and a can of balls with me," she said. "I'd forgotten what it was like, it's so long since I've been here. Then we just drove by."

"My game is golf," the wealthy art collector grumbled. "But since I was making an exhibition of myself when we arrived in town, I didn't get a chance to show you the two courses."

By this time two polite, uniformed bellboys had appeared to unload their luggage, and a chubby, short, pleasant-faced man in a brown suit came down the steps, smiling, and grasped Arthur Kulas' hand in a friendly fashion.

"I'm delighted to have you back with us, Mr. Kulas," the middle-aged man said. "We'll have the boys take your things upstairs right away. Your suite is ready." And he turned to beam at Carol.

"This is my nurse, Miss Holly," the retired

51

diplomat said in a weary tone. "The assistant manager of the hotel, Timothy Ryan."

Timothy Ryan at once began shaking Carol's hand as vigorously as he had that of her patient. "You'll like it here, Miss Holly," he said in warm fashion. "We have lots of activity all through the summer season."

"Ryan, do stop pumping my nurse's hand that way," Arthur Kulas said in his most cutting manner. "It tires me just to watch you." And he glanced toward the rear of the station wagon where the boys were unloading the baggage. "And tell those young men to handle my baggage gently. Those locked trunks contain the materials I use in my lectures. Some of the items are priceless."

Timothy Ryan at once dropped Carol's hand and, looking crushed, hurried to supervise the bellboys. "Gently, lads," he said. "You heard what Mr. Kulas said. He has some very valuable things in his bags."

Arthur Kulas watched the proceedings bleakly. "Perhaps I should have stayed at the hospital," he said.

Carol looked at him anxiously. "Are you feeling unwell again?"

He gave her an icy look. "Please remember this for the future, Miss Holly. When I feel unwell I will inform you. That is why you are here, not to plague me with nonsensical questions."

At last the baggage was all carried inside, and they made their way through the foyer to the large inner lobby where the elevator was located. Their suite was on the third floor. Carol's room had a door leading to the suite as well as direct access to the corridor. Getting the luggage inside was a major task, and afterward Arthur Kulas sat exhausted in an easy chair, directing Carol as she unpacked his personal belongings. The materials for his show remained in the locked trunks and suitcases he'd had the bellboy install in one of the large closets.

"I think I'll go downstairs for dinner," he announced with a determined look.

Carol, who'd just completed unpacking, regarded him with some dismay. "The doctor didn't recommend that."

"I hardly know that young doctor," her patient said dourly. "So what can he possibly know about me?"

"He knows you were very ill this afternoon, and so do I," she said firmly. "You really shouldn't overdo it this evening."

"I think dining downstairs will be good for me," Arthur Kulas insisted. "I shall expect you to join me. And please don't show up in a uniform and nurse's cap. I don't want people to regard me as an invalid. And I like to see young women dressed attractively."

She smiled. "My wardrobe is limited. I expected to wear my uniforms a good deal of the time. But I'll do my best."

She selected a plain linen dress and wore a single strand of pearls with it. Arthur Kulas had changed to a black suit and looked somewhat rested as they made their way into the dining room. The French head waiter knew him from previous summers and welcomed him effusively.

"I'd like my usual table on the verandah, Alfred," the retired diplomat said. "And Miss Holly will be at my table regularly."

Alfred, a balding, urbane little man, nodded pleasantly and led them through the large dining room to a table for two at a window overlooking the gardens.

The food was reasonably good, and her patient appeared to be on his best behavior. Carol relaxed.

Arthur Kulas eyed her across the table. "Do you like the dinner music?" he asked.

She'd only been vaguely aware of it, but now she realized an orchestra in the main dining room was playing a program of Viennese waltzes. "It's very pleasant," she said.

"One of the best things about the place,"

was her patient's comment. "Andy Kerr, the leader and saxophone player, is from Glasgow. I've had many a chat with him. You'll meet him later."

Carol was finishing her coffee when a striking-looking dark-complexioned young woman came by their table, followed by an older woman who was also very dark. The girl was wearing a lovely white cocktail dress that contrasted with her dusky skin. A diamond pin sparkled on her dress and was matched by diamond drop earrings and and a dazzling array of rings on her fingers.

The dark girl paused at their table to give Arthur Kulas a delighted smile, revealing perfect white teeth against the deep crimson of her lovely lips. "Mr. Kulas! What a surprise to meet you here again this year."

The retired diplomat lost his aplomb for a moment. He rose from his chair, napkin in one hand, while he took the girl's diamond-bedecked fingers in the other.

"I'm afraid I don't recall you," he confessed.

The girl uttered a small musical trill of laughter. "Oh, come now, Mr. Kulas," she said. "You can't have forgotten me that easily. We only met once, I'll admit. But we had such a lovely talk."

He smiled. "I can only be pleased that you

have remembered me. Are you going to be here the entire season?"

"That depends," the dark girl said. "I'm Mimi Gamal, since I suppose you've also forgotten my name. And this is my Aunt Rachel, who is staying here with me."

Arthur Kulas bowed deeply to the aunt and then introduced Carol without mentioning she was his nurse. The dark girl, apparently under the impression Carol must be some relative, was especially nice to her. After a few minutes more the two moved on.

Kulas sat down with a baffled expression on his classic features. "That's most unusual," he said. "How could I forget a girl like her?"

"She is striking," Carol agreed.

He sighed bleakly. "Clearly a sign of my general disintegration. I shall soon be an elderly party mumbling into his soup and recognizing no one."

Carol smiled. "I don't see that. And Miss Gamal did remember you."

"So she did," he said, looking pleased. "I must have impressed her favorably."

"I'm sure you did. She's very dark, isn't she? What nationality would you say she was?"

Arthur Kulas considered. "The name Gamal suggests she could be Turkish. But she's too beautiful for a Turkish woman. More apt to be of mixed blood. They are always the loveliest women."

"She certainly seemed glad to see you."

"I must find out more about her," he said. "Timothy Ryan will be able to fill me in on her background. It's his business to know everyone here."

After dinner, he insisted they go out to the front lobby, where the chubby Timothy Ryan was seated at his assistant manager's desk. He rose at once to greet them. Arthur Kulas told him about the dark girl and asked when she'd been at the hotel before.

"Never," Timothy Ryan said.

"Never?" Kulas echoed, his world-weary face showing surprise.

"No. This is her first visit," Timothy Ryan said, smiling. "Pretty, isn't she?"

"Yes, she is," Arthur Kulas agreed in a preoccupied tone. "She claims to have met me here last year. In fact, she stopped at my table to introduce herself to me again. Yet I don't remember her at all. And now you say she wasn't a guest of the hotel last year."

"She wasn't," Timothy Ryan said. "But perhaps you met somewhere else. She must know you or she wouldn't bother to introduce herself. Both she and her aunt are perfect ladies and extremely reserved."

Carol's patient nodded. "That's probably it," he said, and let it go at that.

The aging diplomat surprised Carol by saying, "I think I'll go back to my suite. It's been a long and tiring day."

Carol nodded. "It has. And it's time for your evening hypo and medicine. Also, don't forget the doctor is coming by."

"I don't need him!" he protested, becoming obstinate again.

"He'll be coming anyway," she said.

Upstairs, he relaxed a little and settled down to listen to some concert music on the radio. After Carol had attended to his medications, she sat with a magazine waiting for Dr. Bill Shaw to arrive.

The phone in the suite rang, and she went over and answered it. It was the young doctor, and she told him he could come up at once. Then she let her patient know he was on the way.

Arthur Kulas turned off the portable radio he had on the table beside him. "He'd better not make a lot of fuss and try to put me in the hospital," he said. "I feel all right."

The young doctor agreed. After he'd finished his examination of the patient, he said, "As long as you take your medicine regularly and don't skip meals, you should coast along without any trouble."

The former diplomat glared at him. "I already know that."

"I'll come by occasionally to see Miss Holly isn't having too many problems with you," Dr. Bill Shaw said with a twinkle in his serious blue eyes.

The patient asked the doctor abruptly, "You play tennis?"

"Yes, I do," he admitted with raised eyebrows.

"When you do come by, I wish you'd play a game of tennis with Miss Holly. She's looking forward to playing and has no partners lined up as yet."

"She'll not be having any trouble finding partners," Dr. Bill Shaw said with a smile. "I'm sure of that. But I'd enjoy playing."

"I'm pretty rusty," Carol said shyly. "I haven't played in quite a while."

"I don't get in as many games as I'd like, either," the young doctor said. "Being the only doctor in a place like this doesn't allow you much free time."

"If you two want to go on discussing tennis, I wish you'd find somewhere else to do it," Arthur Kulas snapped. "I want to listen to the concert on my radio." And he turned the portable radio on loudly.

Carol gave the doctor an amused glance,

and she and the doctor went out into the corridor. When she'd closed the door, she said, "You mustn't mind his abruptness. He's really very nice."

"So Timothy Ryan has assured me," Bill Shaw said with a faint smile. "So far I'm not convinced."

"He's not used to being ill. It frightens him."

"It does most people. Have you been his nurse long?"

"Only a few days, as a matter of fact," she said. "But I feel I've gotten to know him fairly well."

"I understand you're a Canadian from Saint John," Dr. Bill Shaw said. "Did you come here much before you went to the States?"

"Only a couple of times with my father," she said. "And then we went to the Crest for lunch. A big resort hotel like this didn't fit my father's budget."

He laughed. "It wouldn't fit mine either. But I come for dinner once in a while. And I enjoy the dancing."

"I think it's wonderful here," Carol agreed happily. "It's a small world in itself. And hardly any of the patrons are from the area. All the car licenses I've seen have been from the United States and Upper Canada."

"Where the wealth is," he pointed out. And then, after a moment's awkward hesitation, "I have the rest of the evening free. Would you care to go across to the Casino for some dancing?"

She hardly knew what to say. But since her patient didn't need her immediate attention, she could see no harm in accepting the handsome young doctor's offer.

She said, "I'd like to go. The orchestra sounded very good at dinner."

"They have an extra man for dancing," he said as they headed down the corridor to the elevator. "A big fellow called Westy who plays a mean bass. He turned up here last month and rented a place at Chamcook Lake a few miles from here. And then he applied for a job with the band on dance nights."

"He's not one of the hotel unit, then?"

"No. That's why he doesn't play in the dining room. He's a friendly person, but a little on the weird side. His wife is a looker, but she's hard as nails, like the gunmen's molls you see in the movies. She came into my office to have a bad cut on her arm dressed. She got it cleaning up the old summer place they rented. And she told me she's a bartender in some Florida club during the winter."

Carol laughed. "She sounds different."

"She is. You'll see her at the Casino some time. You can't miss her. Young, blonde and hard, pointed face. She seems to be a friend of one of the hotel guests, Mimi Gamal. They're together a lot."

The mention of the dark girl caught Carol's interest. "Do you know Miss Gamal?"

He nodded. "You bet. She's a patient of mine."

CHAPTER FOUR

Carol found this hard to believe. "She certainly doesn't look ill."

"She's not, in the usual sense of the word," the young doctor said. "But she is allergic to certain flowers that grow in this area. And the hotel has these enormous gardens. I've had to prescribe antihistamines for her."

"She seems very nice."

"She is. Sort of a mystery type. Claims she lives in New York most of the time. But she's actually a Lebanese. Her aunt doesn't speak any English at all."

The elevator arrived, and this ended their discussion of Mimi Gamal. When they reached the ground floor they left the hotel and walked down the sidewalk past the row of parked cars toward the Casino building, which was brightly lighted.

"I'll stop by my car and get rid of this bag," Bill Shaw said, holding up his medical bag.

"Where are you parked?"

"Just by the Casino," he said.

He unlocked the trunk of his small black sedan and carefully put the bag inside it. Then he locked it again. "You can't be too careful," he said as they started up the wooden steps to the verandah of the Casino. "I carry a lot of drugs in that bag, and it could be a temptation for a few people around here."

Carol glanced at him in surprise. "You mean there are addicts in the area?"

"I know for a fact a few of the youngsters working for the hotel have been experimenting with LSD and some other pretty potent drugs. It seems to be the in thing to do."

Alfred, the head waiter, was now supervising the pavilon. He greeted them and gave them a table for two at the back of the big dance area. The room was softly lighted, and there was an amber-hued lamp on their table. Bill Shaw ordered, and they listened to the music for a moment.

The stout Andy Kerr was on the orchestra

stand, leading his band in a pleasant fox-trot medley. The big room with its white-clothed tables placed around the rectangular floor was well-filled. Carol saw plenty of fancy gowns and mink stoles among the females, and the men were all dressed in a fashionable manner, many of them in white dinner jackets.

"Only a few local people come here," the young doctor said. "But a lot of the summer residents who have homes near the lodge come over for dinner and dancing."

"I like it," she said.

"By the way," he told her, "let's not be formal. My name is Bill."

She smiled. "And mine is Carol."

So it became Bill and Carol for the rest of the evening. They danced a good deal, and she discovered he danced very well. The music had a good beat, and this helped. Several times when they danced close to the orchestra, the big burly man playing the bass waved to Bill. Carol took a good look at him. He looked like anything but a musician. His face was square and jowed, and he was tanned a deep brown. He smiled frequently, but there was no humor in the smiles, and his deep-set, small eyes had a cold glitter in them.

When they returned to their table, she

mentioned noticing the bass player.

"I can't decide about Westy," Bill said, glancing toward the orchestra stand where the four players were taking a short rest. "He's a good enough player, but he just doesn't seem the type."

"I've never stayed in a big hotel before," Carol said. "I think it's all very exciting."

"It's a wonderful help to the town," the young doctor pointed out. "The hotel can accommodate from three to four hundred guests and is nearly always full. They have a staff of a third that many to operate it, and they all leave quite a lot of money in the town. Even the hospital benefits."

"Is it a paying proposition?"

"No." He shook his head. "We don't expect it to be. The local and provincial government help underwrite it. And we have only a dozen beds. I handle mostly minor injuries, medical cases and an occasional surgical patient when it seems wise to do the surgery here."

She was interested. "I've done surgical nursing," she said.

He gave her a questioning look. "Then why are you wasting yourself on a routine job like this?"

Carol hardly knew what to say. "I like private duty nursing."

"All a patient like Arthur Kulas needs is a companion or practical nurse. It's only because he has so much money that he can afford a regular nurse. And you could be used to more advantage somewhere else."

"The state hasn't taken over nursing yet," she reminded him. "I have a free choice to nurse whom I like where I like."

"Maybe that will have to be changed," he argued. "Do you realize what a shortage of nurses both the United States and Canada face? The whole world, for that matter. I've had to give up doing any surgery because I haven't been able to keep a proper operating room staff."

"That's too bad," she said. "But why blame me?"

"I'm not," he said. "Yet I hate to see a registered nurse wasting her time on the kind of work you're presently doing."

Carol smiled wryly. "And I don't think it's any of your business."

He smiled back at her across the table. "I'll accept the reprimand. I probably am talking out of turn. But I can't help wishing I had you at the hospital. I'd be able to take an occasional surgical case again."

"I saw a nurse when I was there earlier."

"And she's a good one," Bill Shaw agreed.

"But she can be only so many places at one time."

"Is she the only one you have?"

"No. There are three others, but even when you add the services of the several practical nurses we also employ, it makes a thin crew when spread around the clock."

"I can see that," Carol agreed. "Perhaps the town is too small for a hospital. You should send all your patients to the larger cities."

Bill Shaw shrugged. "I don't think the government would give us support if they didn't feel we were needed. And the shortage of help we face is reflected in the big hospitals as well."

"I know something about it," she agreed. "Boston is no exception."

"Yet you stay on doing private duty?"

"Some of the patients I've taken care of were desperately ill," she said defensively. "And Mr. Kulas is not in good shape. You saw what happened to him this afternoon."

"You should have prevented it by making him eat or at least carrying a chocolate bar or something sweet to give him when you saw the attack coming on."

Carol looked down at the table top. "Don't think I'm not feeling guilty about it," she said. "But I was new on the case, and he's

67

not an easy man to handle."

"Agreed." The young doctor smiled. "I wasn't condemning you. I just mentioned it in case you run into trouble in the future. Anyway, I brought you here to dance, not to lecture you. And the music sounds good." He rose with a friendly expression on his pleasant face and led her onto the dance floor.

As they danced, she noticed the exotic Mimi Gamal seated at one of the tables. With her was a slim blonde girl. The blonde was watching Carol and Bill Shaw with a shrewd expression on her rather thin face. From the description she'd been given, Carol knew this was the wife of the bass player, Westy.

The dark girl and the blonde were watching them so closely Carol began to feel embarrassed. By a quirk of fate, when the music ended they found themselves standing by the large table at which the two girls were seated.

At once Mimi Gamal smiled one of her most seductive smiles and said, "Why don't you two join us for a moment? I'd like Miss Holly to meet my friend Jane Weston."

The blonde's hard face brightened. "You're the girl with Arthur Kulas, aren't you? Westy and I heard him give his lecture in Florida, and we think he's great!"

"He is an interesting man," Carol agreed.

Right then the big, muscular bass player came to join them. He seemed to be literally bulging out of his tuxedo. Bill introduced Carol, and when they were all seated at the table she found herself between the bass player and the young doctor.

Westy at once gave her his full attention. "So you're a nurse?" he asked.

"Yes. Mr. Kulas doesn't like to have people know it. He feels they'll think he's sicker than he is."

The small eyes bored into her. "Then he isn't really very sick?"

"Bad enough," she said quickly. "It's just that he won't admit it."

The big man nodded. "A lot of old guys are like that. Well, it should do him a lot of good to be down here."

"I hope so," she said.

Westy didn't seem to stop monopolizing her attention. "Kulas gives a swell lecture," he said. "And all that stuff he brings out on stage! Wow! I'd hate to say how much it would be worth!"

"A lot, from what he says. He has most of it with him. He's planning to give at least one lecture here."

"No kidding!" This seemed to be of great

interest to the big bass player. His face lit up with a smile as he turned to his wife. "Did you hear that, honey? Kulas has all his stuff with him, and he's going to put on that 'Caravans and Costumes' lecture here."

Jane Waston's hard features registered pleasure. "I told you we'd made no mistake coming to St. Andrews this summer."

"Don't tell Mr. Kulas we were asking about him," Westy said. "I might make him feel self-conscious, and then he wouldn't do his show."

"You needn't worry about that." Bill Shaw laughed. "He's very egotistical. I'm sure he likes attention."

Westy gave a deep sigh, and his dress shirt bulged more than ever. "I sure would like to get a look at those silks and satins he uses in his lecture. I mean a close look." The small eyes were fixed on Carol. "Some of the relics he uses for props are really out of this world. If you ever have a chance to show them to me at close range, I'd be much obliged."

She felt distinctly uneasy. There was something in the intensity of his manner she didn't understand. And she had the scary feeling that behind all this casual talk there was a pattern, an evil pattern.

She said, "I haven't even seen the things

70

myself. The bags are locked and stored in the suite. I expect when he's rested he'll sort the things over."

"You bet he will," Westy said enthusiastically, a crafty smile crossing the square face. He placed a huge hand on Carol's shoulder. "And, Baby, if I should just happen by then, who knows? I might get to enjoy some of that precious stuff."

"Westy, you're letting yourself get carried away," his wife said sharply. She jerked her head toward the orchestra stand. "Anyhow, it's time you were back on the job."

The big man looked frustrated and confused. He rose, telling Carol earnestly, "Now don't forget what I said!"

When he'd gone, the hard-faced Jane smiled an indulgent smile. "You mustn't mind him, honey. He's like a big boy. Sometimes he just sort of goes out of control."

Carol was saved from having to make a reply as the orchestra resumed and Bill invited her to dance again. They excused themselves and left the other two women alone at the table.

Bill smiled down at her as they danced. "What you think of them?"

"They're different," she said.

"I'll go along with that," he agreed as they

moved about with the other dancing couples.

"I can't imagine why they're so interested in Mr. Kulas and the things he uses in his show," she worried.

"Well, he is a colorful character."

"I know," she said. "But I can't forget he's had several robberies in Boston."

Bill Shaw looked surprised. "You don't really think these people could have anything to do with that?"

"I suppose not," she said dubiously. But she couldn't shake off an odd premonition.

The dance ended at midnight, and Bill Shaw saw Carol back to the hotel and to the door of her room. The high-ceilinged corridors were silent at the late hour, so they talked in low voices as they said their good nights.

"I'll let you know when I have some free time," Bill Shaw said. "And if you can manage it, we'll have a game of tennis."

"I'd like that," she told him.

He smiled. "If you get bored with your patient, I can always find a job for you at the hospital."

"I don't think that's apt to happen," she told him.

"It's been a good evening," he said. "I hope we can repeat it."

"I hope so," she said, her eyes shining.

Then, quite unexpectedly, he took her in his arms and kissed her. When he let her go, he said, "That wasn't just a casual gesture on my part." And without waiting for her reaction, he was on his way.

Arthur Kulas was sitting in a wooden lawn chair sunning himself as he watched two portly men solemnly occupied in a putting contest on the ninth hole green. It was the fourth morning after their arrival at the Mic-Mac Lodge, and the retired diplomat was almost back to his usual spry condition. He was wearing a cream-colored flannel suit, a cap to match and a red plaid cravat with a dark gray shirt.

He turned to Carol, who was sitting beside him, and said, "Both of those fellows are bores. They're so busy telling me their opinions they'll never listen to a thing I have to say."

She smiled. "I'm glad to see them putt. They need the exercise."

"Changing their cuff links from one shirt to another would be exercise to those two," he said disgustedly. "Look at those stomachs! I have never had a stomach!"

"You've been lucky," Carol told him.

"I've been nothing of the sort," the retired

diplomat said, sitting up indignantly. "I've been careful to diet and get exercise."

"Mr. Ryan says he both diets and exercises, and he keeps on adding weight."

He glared at her. "Timothy Ryan is not bright. He seems to have only one idea, and it's wrong."

Carol could see that her patient was much better. He'd rarely been in such a sarcastic mood. With him it was a good sign. She said, "I had a nice game of tennis this morning with Dr. Shaw."

Arthur Kulas frowned. "I'm aware of that. I watched you from the Casino verandah, and while I was sitting there a most disquieting thing happened."

"Oh?"

"A strange mooselike creature drove up in a truck and carried a bass fiddle up the steps and into the Casino. He kept staring at me oddly and stumbled twice on the steps. I hoped he would crash through the fiddle, but he didn't."

"That must have been Westy, the bass player. He only joins the orchestra for the dances," she explained.

"I knew I hadn't seen him before," her patient said. "And I'm rather glad I hadn't. Anyway, every time I looked around he was lurking in the doorway, peering at me in a most upsetting fashion. I think he must be a lunatic."

"He's just odd," Carol said. "I think a lot of musicians are."

"He's carrying it to extremes," Arthur Kulas huffed. "If he continues to annoy me, I'll complain to Timothy Ryan."

"I've met him at the dances," she said. "As a matter of fact, he and his wife are friends of Mimi Gamal."

He raised his eyebrows. "That dark beauty! I find that astounding. She's a lovely girl." Leaning on the arm of his chair, he went on confidentially, "It's all straightened out about our previous meeting."

"Then you did meet?"

"Right here in the hotel," Arthur Kulas said with a pleased expression.

"But Timothy Ryan said she wasn't a guest here last season."

"Timothy Ryan is an idiot!" her patient said, returning to a favorite theme. "She was the guest of a guest here. Stopped by for a few hours, you know. And it was then she was introduced to me. Fine girl! I knew she wouldn't have said she'd met me here if it wasn't so."

Carol thought it all pretty confusing. "I'm glad you were able to get at the truth," she said.

He smiled. "I intend to go over the next night there is dancing. She's very anxious to tango with me."

Carol showed alarm. "That's a strenuous dance," she warned him.

"I'm not a doddering cadaver, Miss Holly," he said primly. "I can still put one foot in front of another, and that is chiefly what a tango consists of."

"You'd better ask Dr. Shaw first."

"Dr. Shaw makes an excellent tennis partner for you," the retired diplomat said coldly. "And that is where his usefulness ends, from my point of view. I have to discuss the matter of my lectures with Timothy Ryan," he told her as he got up. "I'll see you at lunch." And he left her to go across the driveway and up the front steps of the hotel to find the assistant manager.

Carol sat alone in the warm sunshine, vaguely aware of the two stout men still engaged in their putting game. She was still dressed in her tennis whites, and she had an impulse to go back to the courts and practice on the backboard for a while. Anything would be better than sitting around doing nothing.

She rose from the chair and started down the sidewalk to the Casino and the tennis courts beyond. At the moment none of them were being used.

As she approached the Casino, she saw two figures just inside the doorway of the big building. Westy and Mimi Gamal were standing facing each other, engaged in earnest conversation. The big bass player seemed in an angry mood, and Mimi, in abbreviated shorts, stood with a hand on her hips coolly listening to him.

Carol hurried by, pretending she hadn't seen them. At the same time she wondered what was going on between the two.

She let herself through the hinged wire door into the tennis court area and closed it after her. She went to the second court and began to work at the backboard, trying to correct some of her weak points. She became absorbed in what she was doing and gradually forgot about the other things that had been nagging her. It was getting really warm in the noonday sun, and she found herself tiring. She'd just missed an especially easy ball and had paused in annoyance when she heard someone coming up behind her.

"You can do better than that," a voice said.

And since the voice seemed familiar, she turned quickly to find herself facing a handsome, tanned young man in tennis shorts. It was Walter Pitt, the fellow with whom she'd had such an argument on the street in Boston.

Chapter Five

Carol stared at him in silent dismay for at least thirty seconds before she cried, "Oh, no! It can't be!"

He grinned. "I had no idea you'd be so overjoyed to see me."

"I'm not overjoyed," she corrected him. "I'm shocked! I don't believe it!"

Walter Pitt spread his hands. "Don't you have any respect for fate or coincidence or whatever you want to call it? Have you no confidence in the stars and their guidance?"

"The stars haven't anything to do with this," she said angrily. "You started following me on Beacon Street, and you've kept it up all the way to Canada."

He looked amused. "As I remember, you were about to call a policeman."

"I still can," she warned him.

"Now just a minute," he said, raising a placating hand and taking a couple of steps to bring himself closer to her. "Fair is fair. You should be willing to let me explain."

"What is there to explain?" she demanded indignantly. "You're a low type who goes around tailing innocent girls."

"Not really," he said in a calm tone that only increased her anger. "In the first place, I stopped following you in Boston, if you'll bother to remember. You didn't tell me you were coming here. How could I possibly have found out?"

"You probably have secret agents," Carol accused him.

He looked at her hard. "You've been seeing too many spy films."

"Have you the nerve to tell me this meeting is strictly accidental?"

"That's just what I was going to tell you."

"I don't believe it," she said firmly.

"We're back where we started. Look, I advertised that I'd found the purse, and a girl claimed it. I decided I would drive down to Canada for a holiday, and I got here yesterday. I'm staying at the Crest Hotel on the main street for a week or two, and they have tennis privileges for their guests here. I came up to see if I could find someone to play with, and I saw you bouncing balls on the backboard. End of the story."

"I'm glad you call it a story," she said grimly. "That's what it has to be."

"If you'd think this out coolly rather than allowing your emotions to rule you, you'd realize you're doing me a great injustice," the young man said earnestly.

Carol was beginning to weaken, but she was still unconvinced. "I must have mentioned I was coming here and forgotten about it," she insisted.

"And you think I'd drive more than four hundred miles on the chance I'd see you," he said, slightly indignant himself now. "Young lady, you are nuts."

This got through to her. She began to relent a little.

"I don't want to seem unreasonable," she said.

"Thanks," he said bitterly.

"I suppose it is possible that you came here entirely on your own, without knowing I was here."

"Along with hundreds of others. Remember that. I'm only one tourist in a town filled with them."

She looked at him with an embarrassed smile. "I'm sorry I snapped at you the way I did."

Walter Pitt stared at her in wondering admiration. "I never thought I'd live to see the day."

She shook her head. "Don't blame me. You tried picking me up on the street. Naturally I'm suspicious of you."

"I didn't try to pick you up, dear lady," he said with an obvious effort to hold back his anger. "I found a purse. Remember?"

"I'm not likely ever to forget." She laughed. "You made me run almost all the way home. I was sure you were some kind of madman."

"So now we understand each other. Okay?"

"All right," she said in a friendly tone. "I'm glad to see you again, and I hope you enjoy your holiday."

"Do you like it here?" he asked, looking at the Mic-Mac Lodge high on its hill. "Isn't it pretty expensive?"

"My way is paid," she informed him. "I'm a nurse, here with a patient."

He glanced at her. "Lucky you! Does your patient take much time?"

"No. He's not that ill," she said.

The young man showed interest. "He?"

"He's an elderly man," she said "Quite feeble."

Walter Pitt smiled. "Well, that's comforting. For a moment I pictured you in the clutches of some young wolf."

"Now who's been seeing too much television?" she wanted to know.

"Since I'm here dressed to play, why not have a game?" he asked.

She looked at her wristwatch. "It will have to be a quick one. I'm due to join my patient for lunch."

"We have time," he assured her. "Let's try court one. It looks in the best shape."

Walter Pitt turned out to be an excellent tennis player, better than Bill Shaw. He beat her six to one.

They came together breathlessly after the set. "You're too good for me," she said.

"No such thing," he assured her. "Give us a few more games together, and I'll be fighting to hold my own. You play well for a girl."

"Thanks," she said.

They were outside the courts now. He halted as they came to the sidewalk leading to the hotel. "When will I see you again?"

"I don't know," she said. "You're the one who keeps turning up in strange places."

"Maybe I'll see you at the pool this afternoon," he suggested. "The Crest gives its guests swimming privileges here also."

"It's a wonder they don't send you to us for room and board as well," she said with an amused smile.

The young man responded genially. "They do send you their overflow," he joked. "Isn't that fair enough?"

"I may see you by the pool then," she said. "I sometimes go down. It depends on Mr. Kulas."

"Your boss?"

"Yes. Arthur Kulas. He's quite famous for his lecture presentations. You may have heard of him."

"Sorry. I'm not much of a lecture bug," the young man said. "If I don't see you at the pool, I'll come around in the morning for tennis. About eleven?"

"Eleven would be fine," she said.

When she went down to the dining room to join Arthur Kulas for lunch, he gave her a dour glance as she seated herself opposite him.

"You're late," he said.

"I know," she apologized. "I played an extra game."

"You found yourself a new partner," the retired diplomat said. "I was watching from my window."

She knew she was blushing. "It's a boy I met in Boston. I knew him before I came here."

Arthur Kulas raised his eyebrows. "Indeed?" he said. "You seem to attract young men. I trust you're not going to allow a biological urge to get you into trouble."

"I didn't think you minded me playing," she said seriously.

"I don't mind you playing; what worries me is the possibility of your playing around," he told her. "That I won't condone. You may be interested to learn that I've arranged with Timothy Ryan to give my lecture in the Casino three times over the summer. I'll do it at two-week intervals. So we must start to open the cases and go through the materials this afternoon."

Carol knew this meant she'd have no session at the swimming pool. Therefore she wouldn't see Walter Pitt again until morning.

When they finished lunch, she went upstairs with Arthur Kulas and began the inspection of the luggage devoted to his lecture things. He took delight in holding up the exquisite brocades, satins and metal textiles for her examination.

"You'll never see this kind of cloth produced in America," he said triumphantly. "Some of the items in my collection are unique. They will never come from another loom or weaver. For that reason they're priceless and will become yearly more valuable."

Carol found his rug collection interesting, especially the ones given him by the unfortunate Sousa. They were colorful and rich in design. Two of them showed a pattern in mosaic style featuring slaves carrying gifts to an enthroned king. The other one was of curious design, with Arabic lettering interspersed with strange signs in a confusing manner.

"I have no idea of the significance of this one," Arthur Kulas admitted. "It escapes me."

The afternoon went by quickly, and they were almost ready to start repacking the precious items when the phone rang sharply. Carol answered it as she always did when she was in the suite and recognized Timothy Ryan's voice at the other end of the line. The chubby man seemed to be in an agitated state.

"I'm glad to get you, Miss Holly," the little man said. "There's been a dreadful accident back of the hotel. Andy Kerr's son ran into a parked truck with his motorcycle. I don't know what caused him to do it, but he's badly hurt and bleeding. I've called the hospital, and they're sending their station wagon right away. But I thought you might help in the meantime."

Timothy Ryan might have gone on endlessly if she hadn't interrupted. "I'll be right down!" She replaced the receiver to tell a startled Arthur Kulas, "There's been a bad accident. The orchestra leader's son. They need me." And she rushed out of the room and down the hall.

Ryan had sent the elevator up to get her,

and the girl was waiting with the elevator door open. It took only a minute or so to reach the lower floor, where an agitated Timothy Ryan was waiting to grasp her arm.

"Come with me," he said, and hurried her to a side exit just opposite the elevator. The little man raced her along a narrow walk and down over a rolling hill to the back street behind the hotel where the accident had taken place.

A small circle of people were gathered around a figure covered with a blanket. She saw the stout Andy Kerr kneeling by the motionless form of his injured son. As Carol came rushing up, he gave her a pleading look.

"Try to help him," the orchestra leader implored her in a low voice.

She nodded and, kneeling, quickly uncovered the accident victim. What she saw made her ill. His face was a pulpy bleeding mess, with a terrible cut by his left eye. The left leg was also lacerated to an alarming degree and bleeding badly. It looked as if it might be broken in one or more places.

"Handkerchief, tie, anything I can use to halt the bleeding?" She glanced up at the silent onlookers. Andy Kerr already had both a tie and a large white handkerchief available for her. She took them and went to work.

In a moment she had noticeably slowed the bleeding. And by the time she'd started to give some attention to the battered boy's face, she heard the hospital station wagon come to a tire-screeching halt. There followed a rush of running footsteps, and then Dr. Bill Shaw was on his knees beside her, making a hasty examination of the accident victim.

"Glad you got here," he said. "That tourniquet has helped. We'll have to get him to the hospital without delay." He gave her a glance. "Come along. I'll need you."

She hesitated only a moment. It was possible her patient would be annoyed at her leaving without permission. But Bill had said he might need her, and the boy's life might depend on how things went at the hospital. With or without permission, she had no choice but to go.

She followed the stretcher into the station wagon and sat by the injured youth as they made the brief trip to the hospital. The boy was unconscious, or his suffering would have been unbearable.

When they reached the hospital, Bill had the boy sent to the operating room at once. He turned to Carol.

"I'll want a scrub nurse," he said. "Miss Caine can manage the anesthesia if you'll scrub for me. Are you game?"

She nodded. "I'll need a gown."

"There are some in the closet of the dressing room," he told her.

Minutes later they were washing side by side in the stainless steel sinks, ready to don gowns and masks and enter the modest operating room of the St. Andrews Hospital in an attempt to save the life of the orchestra leader's son.

The dependable, sour-faced Nurse Caine was already at the controls of the anesthesia machine. A circulating nurse had prepared the boy for surgery and had the instrument rack ready. Carol made a quick survey of the white-walled room. It was the first time she'd been in it.

Bill spoke in a crisp professional manner. "We'll tackle the face and head injuries first. They are the most serious."

Carol realized that he was right. Her tourniquet would hold back any dangerous bleeding of the leg. This would give them time to proceed with repairs to the pitifully damaged face of the boy.

"We'll need a transfusion," Bill Shaw said. And he asked the circulating nurse, "You have the type?"

"Yes. That's done," she said.

Bill was studying the great cut in the lad's cheek. "It's the eye that is most urgent," he said quietly. "We must try to save it."

Carol was at his side to pass the instruments he required quickly and without error. It had been some time since she'd worked in surgery, but under tension she recalled all the familiar techniques. She couldn't fail Bill or the boy now.

She watched with fascinated eyes as the young doctor's rubber-gloved hands proceeded to attack the damage around the eye and make neat repairs. After a while he hesitated just a moment.

"It looks better," he said. "We should be able to save the sight. There's concussion. But he ought to come out of that in due time on his own. I see no hint of crushed bone or pressure. So now we'll take care of the rest of that cut." And he proceeded to stitch it neatly. The work in that area was done.

Carol was already feeling dreadfully weary. She steeled herself as they began the task of repairing the messy leg damage. At first glance it looked like a hopeless task. But again Bill worked steadily, methodically, until a pattern of reconstruction began to emerge. Carol couldn't help but admire his talent as a surgeon.

Only the hissing of the anesthesia machine broke the silence as Bill completed the final repairs to the terribly damaged leg of the orchestra leader's son. Then it was over. He nodded for the boy to be wheeled out.

When they were alone, Bill took off his mask. His serious young face wore a look of satisfaction. "Thank you," he said to Carol. "You realize you did a good afternoon's work."

"Will he recover?" she asked.

"I hope so," he said. "It all depends on the head injuries. I'm gambling that he will come out of the concussion all right. We've saved his eye and his leg."

"You were wonderful," she said.

"I was clumsy a good deal of the time," he said with a sigh. "But we managed. I may be criticized for not rushing him to St. Stephen. But I didn't think we could risk even the half-hour it would take to get there. To take the hour or more needed to get to Saint John would have been out of the question."

"You should be commended, not blamed," she said.

He looked at her with resignation. "A lot will depend on whether the boy recovers or not. If things go wrong, there always has to be a scapegoat. But we needn't worry about that yet." He paused. "You know you belong in an operating room."

"It's been a long time," she faltered.

"You have the ability," he went on. "So few people have a genuine talent for surgery. You were right there when I needed you."

She smiled wanly. "I was terribly frightened."

"It didn't show," he assured her. "Now I must go tell his father how things stand. He'll be waiting outside."

After he left, she remained to help Nurse Caine clean up the operating room.

When they had finished, the stout nurse smiled at her. "It was lucky for us you were available. Otherwise the doctor would have had to send that poor lad all the way to St. Stephen."

"I'm glad I was able to help," Carol said.

"Come again," Nurse Caine suggested with a new friendliness.

By the time Carol had changed back to her afternoon dress, Bill had talked with the injured boy's father, and all the crowd had gone except Andy Kerr himself, who waited dejectedly on a bench in the lobby. The little Scot looked forlorn and lost.

Carol paused by him as she made her way out. "Don't take too much out of yourself,

Mr. Kerr. Your son has a good chance."

"Aye." The curly-headed orchestra leader nodded. "So the doctor says. But it's given me a fair start. I can't seem to do anything but sit here and stare at nothing."

"That's normal enough," Carol told him. "You've had a bad shock. You can't expect to get right over it."

The fat face was grateful. "Thanks, miss. What worries me the most is that we're to play tonight. For the dance, you know. And I don't see how I can do it."

"Perhaps they'll let you have the night off," she suggested.

"And leave just the piano, drums and bass," he said with a sigh. "No, that wouldn't do. Not with a house full of guests. It's my job to be there, no matter how I feel, so I suppose I'll have to try."

"Your son may have regained consciousness by then. If that happens, you can be certain he'll be all right."

He nodded. "I'd give a lot to hear that, miss."

"I'm sure it will turn out that way," she told him.

She was on the street before she heard Bill calling her name. He came hurrying out to join her. "Let me drive you back to the hotel," he said breathlessly.

She shook her head. "No. It's only a short walk. I'll enjoy the air. You're busy here."

"You're sure?" he said.

"I am." She smiled. "Thanks for the offer, anyway."

"Tell Mr. Kulas that I'm deeply grateful to him," Dr. Bill Shaw went on. "I intend to phone him and explain that I urgently needed you."

"He'll understand," she said.

"I'll probably not see you tonight," Bill Shaw said. "But maybe we can get some tennis in tomorrow morning."

She nodded. "I'll keep in touch to hear how the boy makes out."

The young doctor looked grim. "Tonight should decide."

When Carol left him, she followed a quiet tree-lined road with a few houses on it that was the most direct route back to the Mic-Mac Lodge. There wasn't much traffic on the road, so even if there was no sidewalk she felt relatively safe. Her mind was filled with the tense events of the afternoon.

She was so occupied with her thoughts she wasn't aware of the sound of a car coming up behind her until it was very close. Then she turned to see a battered blue half-ton truck. It came to a noisy halt beside her, and a smiling moon face with a bushy red beard poked out of the dab window. The face was topped by a nautical cap.

"Hello, my colleen," a soft Irish brogue greeted her. "Is it the hotel you're going to?"

CHAPTER SIX

Carol was somewhat taken aback by the genial manner of the jaunty Irishman grinning out of the cab window at her. She said, "I am going to the hotel. But I prefer to walk, thank you."

He beamed. "Now that's a proper ladylike attitude," he agreed. "But sure you don't have to be afraid of me. And I know who you are — the nurse who came to the aid of that poor lad. I was at the hotel when it happened, delivering my employers' luggage."

This caught her interest. "Oh? I was too upset to notice anything."

"It's a proper heroine you were," the red-bearded sailor man assured her in his easy brogue. "Permit Captain Tim Mullaney of the yacht *Cynthia* to offer his compliments."

"Thank you," she said. She was finding the big round-faced man amusing.

"I'm taking a few other things to the hotel, and you might just as well ride along," Captain Tim Mullaney insisted.

Not wanting to give him the impression she considered herself above riding in a truck, she decided she'd better accept his offer. She smiled. "All right. It will get me to the hotel quicker."

"In two shakes of a lamb's tail," the captain assured her.

He had the door open, and she went around and got in on the worn leather seat beside him. The captain was dressed in shabby navy blue trousers and a colorless sweater. The jaunty cap gave him a certain air of distinction, and there was the pungent smell of pipe tobacco about him. She suspected the bulging pocket of his sweater held a pipe and tobacco pouch.

"We docked only this morning," the captain went on as he headed the rattling truck over the not-so-smooth road. "Came from Machias. Colonel and Mrs. Hooper are staying at the hotel, and I'm living aboard. You'll be meeting the colonel and his lady. A fine, conservative couple. Colonel Bart Cooper is the boss' full name. Before he retired he was a big man in Wall Street. Now he spends the summers sailing off New England and the winters sailing in the Bahamas."

"It sounds wonderful," she said.

The captain nodded. "Indeed it is. I'm a

lucky Irishman from County Clare, and so I have this duck of a job. The boss is a proper gentleman, and his dear little lady, Ellen, is from the South. A proper magnolia blossom of a woman. You'll meet them both! They're friendly for all their wealth."

"The hotel is full of interesting people," she agreed.

"I could be staying there myself," the jaunty Irishman said. "But I like to live aboard. There is only one in the crew, and it gives him some time to leave the ship when I'm there. It works out grand!"

She smiled. "You love the sea?"

"Born and bred on its shore," Captain Tim Mullaney declared. "A cabin boy when I was twelve. There's not an ocean in the world I haven't seen. But this is my favorite berth. And what brings you to this part of the world?"

"I'm here as nurse to a rather prominent man, Arthur Kulas. You may have heard of him."

The captain's moon face took on a serious look. "Now would he be the one who gives those fine lectures, about the Arabs and all?"

She was pleased that he'd recognized her employer's name. "That's the one. How do you come to know about him?"

"Sure we spend a month each winter in Palm Beach, and it was at a hotel there that I saw him. Silks and satins and all kinds of marvelous things he has. You must be more than pleased to work for such a man!"

"He is very interesting," she agreed.

"Now I'd like to make his acquaintance sometime," the man at the wheel said. "I could tell him of a certain adventure I had when sailing the Red Sea. It might make a story for one of his grand lectures."

"I'm sure he'd be interested," she said as the truck came to a halt before the hotel entrance. She hesitated before getting out. "I could mention you to him, if you don't mind."

The Irishman beamed. "Mind? Sure I'd be delighted! Now just a minute, dear colleen." And with that he burst out of the cab and trotted around to open her door for her with a flourish.

She laughed. "Thank you!" And she let him take her hand to help her down.

Hurrying into the lobby, she lost no time getting upstairs to shower and change to a dress suitable for the evening. She knocked on her employer's door first, but there was no reply. He often went downstairs to the cocktail lounge before going in to dine, so this did not surprise her. But she regretted missing him, since she'd wanted to give him a full explanation and apology before dinner. Now it would have to wait.

When she took the elevator downstairs again, she had on a green dress that Arthur Kulas especially liked. It was part of her project to get him in the best possible frame of mind. The hotel was full of talk about the accident, and the girl operating the elevator seemed concerned.

"How is Chuck Kerr?" she asked Carol. "Was the operation a success?"

"I think he'll come around," Carol said. "Dr. Shaw did some wonderful work on him. It's a matter of waiting now."

When she left the elevator, she paused by the cocktail lounge but couldn't see any sign of her employer. She hurried on to the dining room where Alfred, the head waiter, greeted her.

"Ah, yes, Miss Holly," he said. "You will have a different table tonight. Mr. Kulas is entertaining guests. And he mentioned that I should take you to join him." With that he led the way through the crowded dining room.

Arthur Kulas was seated at a circular table on the verandah not far from their regular table for two. With him were an elderly man and woman whom Carol had never seen before. The two men rose as she reached the table, and she was relieved to see that her employer was smiling radiantly.

"This is my nurse, Carol Holly, who so distinguished herself this afternoon," Arthur Kulas introduced Carol grandly as the head waiter hovered nearby, waiting to seat her. Her employer turned to the elderly couple. "I want you to meet some fine new friends I've made, Colonel Bart Hooper and his dear wife, Ellen."

The colonel was bald and tanned, with a shrewd squint in alert blue eyes and a toothy smile. "Enchanted, Miss Holly," he said in a courtly fashion.

His wife Ellen, gray-haired but younger, smiled at Carol. "What a charming girl! But then I knew Mr. Kulas would show exquisite taste in a nurse, as he does in everything else." Ellen Hooper was clearly a sweet little woman, positively dripping Southern warmth. "Honey," she said, "you must sit between the colonel and me. We want to know you, especially the colonel. He has this thing about dark-haired girls."

Carol smiled and let the head waiter make a place for her between the two newcomers to the hotel. Colonel Hooper regarded her with shrewd, twinkling eyes and a toothy smile and reached to take her hand in his and squeeze. He laughed rather loudly for no particular reason. "My wife is right," he said conspiratorially. "I do indeed have a passion for brunettes."

She was a little overwhelmed. The colonel might be old school, but he certainly was a fast worker. The petite Ellen gave her husband a warning glance.

"You mustn't rush this honey child off her feet, sweet," she said in her best Southern lady style. And then, with a gentle look for Carol, she suggested, "Wouldn't you like a martini, dear? I might even join you myself."

It was the colonel's turn to flash a warning look. He suddenly lost the toothy smile. "You have had your quota far before dinner, Ellen. Remember?"

The tiny attractive woman with the short gray hair simpered. "Bart adores bullying me, and I find it so flattering."

Carol was relieved that the waiter arrived to take their orders. Arthur Kulas presided grandly as host and gave very particular instructions about how each dish had to be cooked. But he was in an amiable mood. The Hoopers had worked wonders with his disposition. And no doubt a prolonged session in the cocktail lounge hadn't hurt. Now he was ordering wine and consulting Ellen Hooper on her preferences.

The little lady daintily gestured with a tiny hand. "Just so long as there is plenty of it, dear Mr. Kulas."

Carol was conscious of a surreptitious movement beside her, and before she realized what was happening the elderly Colonel Bart Hooper was holding her hand again.

His blue eyes crinkled in a smile and he laughed loudly. "The hotel is raving about how wonderful you were," he said. "We arrived just about the time of the accident. What excitement!"

"I met your captain, Tim Mullaney," Carol said, hoping he'd soon let her hand go. "He said that he was here when the Kerr boy crashed into the truck."

The colonel showed surprise and released her hand. "You've met Tim Mullaney?"

"Yes. He gave me a lift to the hotel in the truck," she said. "He spoke of you being here and told me he'd heard one of Mr. Kulas' lectures in Florida last winter. He said he enjoyed it very much."

"Did he, now?" her employer said, at once interested.

"Tim is a remarkable man. I don't know what we'd do without him," Ellen Hooper said seriously. "And he's so well educated. He could be an executive if he wished. But he prefers the simple life. Bart and I begged him to stay here at the hotel, but he'd rather be aboard the *Cynthia*."

"Positively!" the colonel said with a nod.

Dinner went well. The retired diplomat did complain about the potatoes, but the captain had them quickly replaced, so that crisis evaporated. The talk around the table was good, and Carol was impressed by the Hoopers' knowledge of music, theatre and art. She realized why they had made so quick a conquest of the sharp-tongued diplomat. They were wonderful people!

Dinner over, they all strolled out into the large lounge. Mimi Gamal and her aunt were seated on the other side of it, and Arthur Kulas quickly excused himself to go over and spend a few minutes with them.

Ellen Hooper studied Carol in her shy fashion. "I do hope you'll attend the dance tonight," she said. "The colonel dotes on dancing, especially the waltz, and I often prefer to remain at the table and rest."

The colonel's shrewd blue eyes twinkled as he gave her his attention. "You will sit at our table, won't you?"

"It depends on Mr. Kulas," Carol said, hesitating.

The elderly man in the smart gray suit dismissed this with a gesture. "But of course he will be joining us, as well."

When Arthur Kulas returned from his conversation with Mimi Gamal, the arrangements were consolidated. The retired diplomat was eager to visit the Casino. "It will be my first evening over there," he said. "And Miss Gamal has promised me a tango."

The colonel eyed the dusky-skinned Mimi greedily and with one of his unexpected loud laughs said, "You must introduce me, old man. I do an excellent tango."

"Now, Bart!" His wife smiled a demure warning and turned to Arthur Kulas. "There is one thing," she said, "I would dearly like to see some of those wonderful brocades and those gold and silver cloths at close range."

The colonel nodded his bald head. "Without a doubt she raved more about your stage presentation and the wonderful things you displayed during it than anything else I can remember."

The diminutive Ellen smiled coyly. "Bart will give my secrets away!"

Arthur Kulas was still in one of his best moods. Expansively he said, "Then why should we delay you the pleasure? Miss Holly and I were going through the trunks this afternoon. They're readily available. Come up to my suite and I'll let you see

103

some of the things now."

Ellen Hooper clasped her hands with delight. "How good of you!"

In the suite, Arthur Kulas opened the most easily accessible trunk and passed around some of the exquisite examples of weaving. The very feel of the fine textiles suggested another and more luxurious age.

"Many of these items cannot be duplicated," the diplomat explained. "The skilled artisans who wove them have died and taken the secrets of their work with them."

Ellen Hooper fondled a gold cloth, and her small face showed awe. "So perfect!" she whispered.

Colonel Bart Hooper gave a toothy smile. "You also have some hammered copper and silver antiques which you use in the show; if I remember correctly. Do you have those along with you?"

The retired diplomat nodded. "Yes. Unfortunately, they are in the rear trunk. There are a variety of precious items, from ancient jars to jeweled figures of cats in which the Egyptians specialized. I'll make sure you have a private showing of them at some later time."

"That's so kind of you, Mr. Kulas," Ellen Hooper said in her sweetest voice as she handed him back the gold cloth. "And you will join us at the Casino and bring darling Miss Holly with you?"

"A great pleasure," Arthur Kulas said with a warm smile on his classic face.

The colonel was already on his way to the door. "We mustn't keep you," he said. "We'll see you at the Casino at ten sharp." And with the shrewd blue eyes on Carol, he added, "I'm looking forward to the first dance, my dear."

At ten, as she walked the short distance between Mic-Mac Lodge and its Casino, Carol was able to hear the sound of the orchestra. And at once she was struck by the lacklustre quality of its playing. The worry of the leader over his injured son was clearly evident in the lagging tempo of the dance music. She could imagine what he was going through at this time.

When she mounted the steps and entered the lobby of the big wooden building, Alfred greeted her with a smile. "You will be at Colonel Hooper's table," the head waiter informed her, and led her across to a large round table which was empty of people at the moment.

She sat down at an empty place and took note of the crowd. The big room was almost filled, and there were a large number of couples on the floor dancing. She picked out Colonel and Mrs. Hooper together, also Arthur Kulas and the hard-faced blonde wife of Westy. In addition, a smiling Walter Pitt in a white dinner jacket held the exotic Mimi Gamal in his arms. They both seemed to be having a good time, and it struck Carol that the young man from Boston had a way of getting to know personable females.

While she was brooding on this, a familiar figure entered the dimly lighted big room and came straight toward her, smiling. It was none other than the pleasant Irishman, Captain Tim Mullaney.

Captain Tim was wearing a trim blue blazer and white flannels. He paused beside her and gave a courtly bow.

"May I have the pleasure of this dance, fair colleen?" he asked in his soft brogue.

"I'd enjoy it," she said.

And a moment later she was being lightly whirled around the floor in the big man's arms. The Irishman beamed down at her. "This is an unexpected pleasure. I hoped you'd be here, but I wasn't sure."

"Are you joining the colonel's party?"

"By special invitation," he said. "I got lonesome aboard the *Cynthia,* so I decided to accept."

"It's very pleasant," she said.

When the music ended, he saw her back

to the table and took a seat beside her. "I hope you don't mind my sitting here. I'm not likely to know most of the others."

At that moment the colonel and his wife returned to the table, and Captain Tim at once rose to his feet. The colonel looked less than pleased to see that the sea-faring man had sat next to Carol. But Ellen at once took over with a gesture of her dainty hand.

"Bart, I know you want to sit beside Carol," she said with one of her sweet smiles. "And I insist that Captain Mullaney sit with me. So you two just change places."

The colonel's shrewd blue eyes lit up, and he hastened to Carol's side with one of his explosive laughs. "My wife can always read my mind," he said happily.

So Carol found herself seated between the colonel and Arthur Kulas. She kept an anxious eye on her patient, since he was already beginning to look weary. She hoped he wouldn't push himself too far. Meanwhile the blonde Jane Weston kept up a running conversation with the retired diplomat.

Carol saw Westy coming down to the table with an excited look on his broad face. Coming up to his wife, but including them all in his gaze, he told them, "Andy has just had word from the hospital. His son has recovered consciousness. Isn't that great news?"

"Indeed it is," Arthur Kulas said at once. "Thanks for telling us."

Westy's tiny eyes showed an icy glitter. "Always glad to bring good news," he said. "And now it's more music."

The band began to play once more, and this time Carol danced with the colonel. For a man his age he was an excellent dancer. And Andy was playing like a different man now. All the relief he felt showed in the lilting beat of the orchestra.

Captain Tim Mullaney danced with the tiny Ellen but he also saw to it that he had several more dances with Carol. Toward the end of the evening she could see that her patient was actually looking ill, and she began counting the minutes until the orchestra ended the affair in the traditional fashion with a rendition of both "O, Canada" and "God Save the Queen," while everyone stood at attention. It was a custom she had missed in the United States, and it always gave her a pleasant feeling of being home.

During the last dance, when she was on the floor with the colonel, Mimi Gamal and the errant Walter Pitt came back into the ballroom to join the dancing couples. It was only then that the young man from Boston saw Carol and, when they passed, tried frantically to catch her eye. Carol revenged herself on him by stonily refusing to look at him.

The captain escorted her back to the hotel and allowed his Irish gallantry to extend so far as to kiss her hand. "Good night, fair colleen," he said. "I shall dream of you under the stars."

She was amused by his blarney and relieved that the evening was at an end.

The phone rang a little after seven in the morning, waking her from a deep sleep. She heard Arthur Kulas on the other end of the line. He was almost incoherent with indignation. "Put on a wrap and come here at once, Miss Holly," the retired diplomat said. "A dreadful thing has happened. I've been robbed again!"

CHAPTER SEVEN

Carol lost as little time as she could putting on a dressing gown and hurrying to the door which led to her patient's suite. She knocked on it, and at once he called out to her to enter.

She opened the door to find him standing there in his bathrobe with a thoroughly upset-looking Timothy Ryan. The assistant manager of the hotel appeared to have dressed in a mad rush. His jacket was not correctly buttoned, and his eyes held a sleepy look.

Arthur Kulas was bristling with rage. "It's a disgrace that this should have happened here!"

Chubby Timothy Ryan stood there unhappily. "But you admit your apartment was broken into three times," he said plaintively. "It ought to be an old story with you."

"This is not my apartment!" the retired diplomat said angrily. "Is this all the protection you give your guests?"

"It seems to me you should have heard whoever it was," the assistant manager said, glancing toward the closet. "They must have made some noise."

"I always sleep with my bedroom door closed," Arthur Kulas said. "And I'm convinced someone put a sleeping potion in one of my drinks last night." He turned his attention to Carol. "Didn't you hear anything either?"

"I'm afraid not," she said. "I was very tired. Did they take many things of value?"

"They broke into the trunk in the rear and concentrated on the art pieces," her employer said. "Fortunately, they weren't very good judges of the worth of the items, for they took some of the less valuable things."

"You should be thankful for that," Timothy Ryan volunteered with a woeful look on his chubby face.

"I do not need you to tell me what I should be thankful for," the wealthy ex-diplomat said angrily. "It's not a disgrace that you're stupid, but it might as well be!"

Timothy Ryan visibly flinched. "No use losing our tempers, Mr. Kulas," he said. "I suppose you'll want me to notify the police."

"Isn't that the usual procedure in a robbery?" her patient asked with disgusted sarcasm. "Or have you some original plan of your own?"

"I didn't know whether you'd want the bother," the assistant manager said. "I mean, you're not feeling well."

"I'll feel a great deal better if I get my property back," Arthur Kulas said with an outraged expression on his classic features. "It gives me no great pride to know I'm a stockholder in this hotel. And I intend to bring the gross neglect in management to the attention of the annual meeting."

"Yes, Mr. Kulas," the little man said forlornly. "I'll notify the police at once." And he went out.

Carol's employer sank down in an easy

chair. "Everybody acts idiotic at one time or another," he moaned. "But the people I have to deal with seem to make a career of it."

"He's really not so bad," Carol said. "This has upset him."

Arthur Kulas glared at her from the chair. "It certainly hasn't done me any good, either."

"Do you want me to help put the remaining things back in the trunk?"

"Of course not," he snapped. "The police will want to look at everything just the way it was left."

"Then I'll give you your morning hypo and medicine to get it over with before the police come," she suggested.

He looked bleak. "If Gabriel was blowing his horn and walls were tumbling all around us, you'd be running after me with a medicine bottle."

All his good humor of the previous night had vanished with the discovery of the theft. Carol listened to his gripes patiently and went about giving him his medications. When she finished, she went back to her own room to shower and dress.

An officer from the local detachment of the Royal Canadian Mounted Police arrived before they had time to get down to breakfast. A nervous Timothy Ryan was with him. The young police officer examined the scene of the robbery carefully and asked a long series of questions. Arthur Kulas soon lost patience with the officer's methods, but the young man accepted it calmly.

"You don't need the history of my life," the ex-diplomat fumed. "Just find how those thieves got a key to my door."

"That's an easy matter," the police officer said quietly. "There are a half-dozen tried and true methods. Every hotel has the same problem."

Timothy Ryan reminded the patient, "They even got into your own home, Mr. Kulas."

"Why do you insist on harping on that?" the unhappy Kulas said.

The police officer turned his attention to Carol and asked her a few questions. After which he closed his note book and told her employer, "We'll do what we can, Mr. Kulas. I can't offer much hope. This has the odor of an inside job. My guess is that someone staying here at this hotel is responsible. Or it could be someone employed here."

"You should question everyone," Arthur Kulas insisted.

The officer looked mildly amused. "I'm

afraid we couldn't do that. But I will make some discreet inquiries." And with that he went on his way.

Carol said, "If we don't go down at once we'll miss breakfast. It's getting late."

Her employer looked disgruntled. "I'm not hungry."

"You must eat," she said. "You've had your medicine."

Breakfast was a gloomy business, with Arthur Kulas hardly saying a word. Carol was afraid to venture any conversation, so she remained silent as well. It was a warm, sunny day, and quite a crowd were gathering around the swimming pool. She wondered if Dr. Bill Shaw might get away for a half-hour of tennis before noon.

She recalled with mild annoyance that Walter Pitt had also asked her about a game around eleven. Well, he'd certainly show his colors last night with the glamorous Mimi Gamal. He'd have some explaining to do about that before she would date him.

When they finished breakfast, she parted company with her employer in the lobby. He announced his intention of changing into a bathing suit and enjoying the pool.

Carol went back upstairs and changed into her tennis outfit. Taking her racquet and can of balls, she went outside to sit on the verandah a few minutes. And she was surprised to find her patient already seated there alone. He hadn't changed into his swimming trunks, but was wearing green plaid slacks and a light sport shirt with short sleeves.

Seeing her, he said, "I changed my mind. I have a headache. I think the sun would be bad for it."

"You're probably right," she agreed. "It is wise of you to rest today. You pushed yourself hard last night. And then there was the robbery to top it off!"

She sat down beside him. "Do you mind if I discuss my own affairs for a moment?"

His distinguished face registered surprise. "What kind of personal affairs?"

"My job for you."

"Well, what about it?" he asked testily.

"You really don't need a full time nurse, Mr. Kulas. I feel wasted in this job."

The retired diplomat's eyes widened. "You must be joking! Of course you know I'm a very sick man."

"You are. But you still don't need me every minute of the day," she protested mildly.

"I can have what I pay for," the wealthy man said. "And I can pay for your services."

"There's more to be considered than

that," she objected. "For instance, the hospital here is dreadfully short of nursing staff."

"I can't help that!"

"But you can do something about it," Carol said. "Give me the afternoons off from one until six. That way I could still look after you and work at the hospital a half-day as well."

Arthur Kulas looked as if he could hardly credit her words. "I don't see that it would work out at all."

"I'm sure it would," she said. "And I will give you credit for whatever the hospital pays me. So you wouldn't be paying me twice."

He frowned. "You sound very intense about this scheme."

"I've been thinking about it almost since the day we arrived here," she said. "And after yesterday I know how badly the hospital needs me."

"What does this Shaw fellow think about your idea?"

"He'd like me to do it."

The retired dipomat sat back in the wicker chair grumpily. "And I suppose if I don't agree, I'll be cast in the role of the villain. You realize that, of course?"

"I don't want to put you in that position," she said.

"Yet you are forcing my hand."

"I wouldn't do that. If you are strongly opposed to the plan, I won't bother you about it any more."

Arthur Kulas glared at her. "All right, do what you like about it. I'm bound to be wrong no matter what I say."

Carol hadn't hoped for such a quick decision on his part. Her pretty face brightened. "I'm sure you won't regret it, Mr. Kulas."

"Don't keep on talking about it," he said wearily. "Just do it. You can begin tomorrow if you like."

"I'll speak to Dr. Shaw," she promised. "I expect to see him at the tennis court shortly."

The retired diplomat gave her a sarcastic look. "So our overworked young medico can take time off for tennis?"

Carol blushed. "He has to have some free time. And he never plays more than one set."

But Arthur Kulas had closed his eyes and was pretending he didn't hear her. She knew it would be unwise to stay there any longer. She had been dismissed. And she was glad of it.

As she neared the tennis courts, she found

some people playing who were strangers to her. But one court still remained free. A glance at her watch told her it was getting near eleven, and she began to worry that Bill Shaw might not have been able to get any free time to play. Sitting on the steps of the Casino, she resigned herself to watching and waiting.

The beep of a familiar car horn caught her attention, and she smiled as she saw Bill's neat black sedan come to a halt close to the tennis courts. She got up from the Casino steps and hurried across to meet him. He was in tennis shorts and looked extremely healthy.

He eyed her happily. "I had to cut some corners to squeeze in this half-hour," he said.

"I'm glad you did."

"You heard about the Kerr boy? He's doing fine."

"Yes. I'm so glad for him and his parents."

"The father has him here with him. His mother is back in Toronto. I can tell you the father was in quite a state," Bill said.

"I know. His music was slow and awful until you phoned him last night."

Bill laughed. "The dancers must have been grateful for that phone call." He opened the door to the courts. "We'll have to begin right away."

Carol went in and then turned as he followed her. "There is one other thing," she said. "Mr. Kulas has given me the afternoons off, beginning tomorrow. So I'll be able to work at the hospital from one until six."

He halted, a delighted expression on his tanned face. "That's the best news this summer. You're going to miss out on all the fun at this resort hotel to work in a hot hospital?"

"I want to do it," she said. "And anyway, there are plenty of headaches here as well as fun. You know Mr. Kulas was robbed last night."

"I didn't," he said, as they walked toward the idle court. "Tell me all the details."

She did briefly. And then they began their game. Bill played very well, but she was in top form. And even though he served a stronger game, she held her own. It ended with the score about even. When the game was over, Bill looked at his wristwatch and frowned.

"That minute hand is a heart-breaker," he said. "I'll have to run. I'm going to change at the hospital."

They quickly left the court and went directly to his car. Before he got in, he hesitated and said, "What are your plans for tonight?"

"Nothing special," she said.

"Suppose I come by when I finish at the hospital," he said. "It won't be early, probably about ten. But we could go for a drive. There'll be a moon tonight, and the bay can be beautiful by moonlight."

She smiled. "I think I'd like it."

"Great." The young doctor looked happy. "I'll pick you up at the front entrance." And he got in the car.

Carol stood there a moment and waved him off. When the car had gone up the hill and turned the corner, she prepared to walk back to the hotel. But before she had taken more than a couple steps, she saw a smiling Walter Pitt come stiding toward her. He was also in tennis whites and carrying a racquet.

He said, "Congratulations. I saw him. In fact, I got here just a minute or so after he did. So I knew I'd lost you as a partner. But I watched you play. You were very good."

"Thank you," she said coolly.

He stood in her way. "Do you have to hurry back to the hotel?"

She eyed him with an air of arrogance. "There's nothing to keep me here."

"There's me."

"I guess I meant that."

He registered pain. "Please!" he said. "That hurt."

"You're much too sensitive."

"I don't think you believe it."

She said, "Did you enjoy the dance last night? Or rather, Miss Gamal's company? You two didn't manage much dancing."

The young man from Boston raised his eyebrows. "So that's it," he said. "You're jealous!"

At once she was indignant. "Why should I be jealous?"

"You didn't like seeing me with the lovely Mimi."

"Why should I be jealous?" she repeated. "I hardly know you."

"People take to me quickly," he teased.

"I think you're an insufferable idiot!" she exclaimed. "And I wish my employer was here. He could think of a lot of wonderful things to call you!"

He raised a protesting hand. "Honestly, I'm not quite that bad. And it was you who brought the Gamal gal up. Last night when I tried to get your attention, you cut me."

"Why not?" she demanded. "You were out on the verandah with her all the early part of the evening. What were you trying to make me — a bonus?"

Walter Pitt shook his head sadly: Then he

grasped her by the arm. "I want you to come over to the steps and listen to me," he said.

"I don't care to hear any nonsense you may have to say!" she protested.

But he led her back to the steps and eased her down in a spot favored by the warm sun. Then he seated himself beside her. He gave her a resigned glance.

"You think I'm some kind of monster, don't you?"

"Freak would be closer," she suggested.

"You never give me a chance to explain anything. No matter what happens, you never let me explain."

"The fact there is always something to explain indicates how way out you are," she said. "I never met a man who attracted trouble the way you do. Not that Mimi Gamal could be described as trouble. She's a very striking girl, and any weak man would be bound to fall at her feet as you did."

It was his turn to look indignant. "I didn't fall at anyone's feet," he said.

She offered him a smug smile. "You were mooning after her like a stricken doe."

The young man from Boston swallowed hard. "That is a distortion of the facts," he said. "As it happened, Miss Gamal was expecting an important phone call. So I walked her back to the hotel after our first dance. I waited for her in the lobby for close to an hour and a quarter until she came down again. Then I took her back to the dance. And when I tried to speak to you, you ignored me."

"It's not a bad story," she admitted.

"It's the truth," he insisted. "Ask her if you like."

"I have other things to think about," she said.

"Like that handsome doctor who frolics around with you on the tennis court when he should be looking after his patients," the young man said in a disgusted tone. "I know who's beating my time with you."

"No one is beating your time with me," she said firmly, "because I have no time for you."

"Doctors make rotten husbands," he said.

"So do would-be writers," she snapped back.

"Doctors are always on call," he said. "Marry me, and I'd be home the whole day long."

"With you that wouldn't be any advantage," she told him.

The young man from Boston smiled. "I like your spirit," he said. "And I figure if I can only make you hate me enough, I'll win out. You know what they say. Hate is the closest thing to love!"

"You're mixing up my emotions," she told him as she got up. "For you I feel disgust."

He got to his feet, too, and shrugged. "Well, at least it's a good positive emotion."

She stared at him in wonder. "You really are crazy, aren't you? And I still think you followed me all the way from Boston."

Walter Pitt smiled. "I've really gotten under your skin, haven't I?"

"I just don't believe it," she said in awe. "It can't be happening." And she hurried down the steps and began striding firmly toward the hotel, tennis racquet swinging in her hand.

He came running after her. "Don't leave me this way!" he protested.

She kept walking quickly toward the verandah. They were passing the swimming pool now, and she felt everyone was watching them. Without turning to look at him, she warned, "Keep following me and I'll scream for help."

"We did that routine back in Boston," he complained. "Give me a break. Will you meet me tonight? There are movies at the theatre in town."

"I'm not interested," she said.

"Please!"

"No," she said. And then, glancing over at the pool, she saw Mimi Gamal's little form clad in a scanty white bikini. The dark girl was poised on the diving board. She said, "There's your friend! Better join her!"

He halted for a moment, and she took advantage of the opportunity to run quickly to the verandah steps. When she looked back, he was walking slowly toward the pool where the glamorous Mimi was already in the water.

With a sigh she went inside. Why was it that Walter Pitt always brought out the worst in her?

His story about the previous night could be true. And yet it had a suspicious ring to it. Why should the exotic Mimi suddenly leave the dance after promising to meet Arthur Kulas there and tango with him? Walter claimed she'd been expecting an important phone call. And she'd gone up to her room and had not returned for more than an hour, at a time when she knew everyone else was at the Casino!

At lunch that day Carol put what she considered a very important question to her employer. "When did you discover the theft?" she asked.

He looked pained. "I think I made that clear enough. When I got up to take something for my headache. I had a sudden feeling that the closet had been disturbed."

"But it needn't have happened then," she pointed out carefully. "After all, you say you didn't hear the thieves. The robbery could have taken place while we were all at the dance. And you wouldn't have noticed when you came in, because you were tired and didn't go near the closet."

Arthur Kulas gaped at her in surprise.

Chapter Eight

"Just what are you trying to prove?" he demanded at last.

She knew it wasn't time yet to divulge her dark thoughts concerning the glamorous Mimi. She had no kind of proof, and the diplomat was so fond of the dusky-skinned girl it was doubtful if he'd listen to any accusations against her.

So she said, "I'm merely trying to establish that the robbery could have taken place earlier in the evening, while we were at the dance."

He considered. "I don't know," he said at last. "It seems to me I'd have noticed as soon as I went into the room."

"Not unless you went over to the closet as you did this morning," she insisted. "And you say you weren't near the closet last night."

"I guess not." He sighed.

"Then that's probably why you weren't awakened by the robbery. It took place before we came back to the hotel."

He eyed her sharply. "If you thought that, why didn't you tell the police this morning?"

"I didn't think of it until later," she said. "I suppose you could phone and tell them."

The retired diplomat looked unhappy. "It's only a guess on your part. And I can't be sure. I don't know whether it's worth telling them or not."

"I think anything that has a bearing on the crime is worth mentioning," she advised him. "You can explain why you didn't say anything about it before."

Her patient sighed. "This thing is really getting me down. My head has felt dizzy all morning."

She smiled. "You did celebrate a good deal last night. You'll probably feel better after you've had your lunch."

She said no more to him about it. But she was doing a lot of thinking. And the more she dwelt on the matter, the more she was convinced that the exotic Mimi might be the thief.

She went to the newsstand and bought a paperback novel which she took out to the verandah. While she was looking for a place to sit and read, someone waved to her from the far end of the long verandah. She at once recognized Colonel Bart Hooper; his wife Ellen and Arthur Kulas were sitting with him. The colonel motioned for her to join them.

Carol went reluctantly, her mind made up to stay with the three only for a few minutes. She was too upset about all that had happened to be in a mood for casual conversation.

Both men rose as she joined the group. Colonel Hooper pulled a chair forward for her. "Sit down with us a moment, my dear," he said with one of his toothy smiles. "We were just discussing the robbery."

"I can't stay long," she said. But she did sit down.

Ellen Hooper smiled demurely at her. "How attractive you looked today on the tennis court. We were watching from the window of our room."

The colonel nodded, his shrewd blue eyes fixed on Carol. "You are at your best in tennis clothes," he said, and reached over to squeeze her hand.

She was wise to his little tricks now and

eluded his grasp without making it apparent. She knew she was blushing and wished that she had not come out on the verandah at all.

"That was the handsome doctor you were playing with, wasn't it?" the gray-haired woman said sweetly.

"Dr. Shaw," her employer filled in for her. "He's looking after me while I'm here."

"And there was another young man," Colonel Hooper smiled, "the one you sat with on the steps for so long. Who is he?"

"He's from Boston," she said. "He's not a guest of the hotel."

"Yet they wander around the grounds," Ellen Hooper said with lifted brows. "Is it any wonder there are robberies? The hotel isn't careful enough about outsiders."

"He does have privileges here," Carol said, defending Walter Pitt. "The Crest Hotel has some kind of arrangement with the Mic-Mac."

"I still say it's wrong," the tiny Southern woman said.

Colonel Hooper uttered one of his raucous laughs. "My wife fancies herself as an amateur detective. Of course she really has no talent for it at all."

Ellen assumed a stubborn expression. "I stand by my theory that whoever committed the robbery was an outsider."

"You could very well be right," Arthur Kulas agreed. He turned his attention to Carol. "This fellow from the Crest Hotel — do you know him well?"

"Fairly well," she said cagily.

"Where did you meet him?" her employer wanted to know.

"In Boston," she said quite truthfully, without giving him the rather peculiar details.

The retired diplomat looked less suspicious. "Then you two are really old friends," he said.

"I suppose you could describe us as that," Carol agreed cautiously.

Ellen Hooper gave the men a reproving smile. "I say it is very wrong of you to quiz this poor girl so about her young man. It's embarrassing, and I wouldn't blame her if she asked you both to mind your own business."

The colonel uttered another of his hooting laughs and told Arthur Kulas, "You see we're stalemated, once the females decide to stick together."

Her employer gave Carol a knowing glance. "You can understand why we are suspicious of any strangers, especially since you believe the theft was committed while we all were dancing."

"I call that very smart deduction, young lady," the colonel said.

She had the feeling he was about to reach out for her hand again, so she quickly got up from the chair. "If you'll excuse me now," she said, "I have to meet someone." And she hurried away down the steps of the verandah.

She walked toward the Casino in a kind of daze, and was only brought back to a state of alertness by a station wagon backing swiftly out from beside the building and passing so close to her it almost grazed her. The experience left her trembling.

Staring to see who the driver was, she recognized the bass player, Westy, at the wheel of the vehicle with his hard-faced wife seated beside him. Neither of them paid much attention to her as they drove up the road and turned a corner out of sight.

So they did occasionally visit the hotel during the daytime! But why today? And what had been their hurry to get away? All these questions plagued Carol as she left the area of the Casino to walk on toward the village. She'd not gone more than a hundred yards when she met the jaunty Captain Tim Mullaney strolling toward her. The bearded young man wore a smile.

As they met, he gave an exaggerated bow. "What good luck I have," he said. "We're always meeting." His eyes peered at her quizzically. "And what causes my fair colleen to look so blue?"

She gave him a despairing smile. "It hasn't been a good day. In fact, it wasn't a good night." And she told him about the robbery.

The tall Irishman gave a shrewd whistle. "Now that's what I call a happening," he observed. "But this Kulas is surely asking for trouble, carrying all those valuable things around with him."

"He does it because of his show," she explained.

"Why not join me for a sail on the *Cynthia?*" Tim Mullaney suggested. "It's a beautiful day, and the sea air will do you good."

She smiled. "Thanks. I just might take you up on that offer."

Shortly afterward she found herself seated in the bow of the *Cynthia* as they moved out into the Bay of Fundy. The red-bearded Tim Mullaney proved a thoroughly entertaining host and regaled her with stories about his sea adventures and his home land of Ireland.

Sitting back with his pipe in hand, he said at last, "But sailing with the Hoopers had been the best of all. They're fine people, and I'd ask nothing more than to go on working for them."

"Probably you will."

He shrugged. "It's hard to say. The colonel is getting older. He may not always want a yacht as large as this. Ellen will do whatever he says."

"She seems very devoted to him."

"And to fine Scotch whiskey, as you may have noticed," Tim Mullaney said with a smile. "But for all that, she is a good little woman and I like her."

"So do I," Carol agreed. She stared back toward the shore and the Mic-Mac Lodge, which stood out on its hill above the bay. The rugged coastline, with its rocks and evergreens and dearth of people, appealed to her.

"Now this Arthur Kulas," the captain said, "does he not have special locks on the closets of his room? With such valuables in those cases, he should."

"He has had locks installed, but they're light ones," Carol confessed. "I doubt if they would hinder any determined thief."

Tim Mullaney drew on his straight-stemmed pipe. "It's true," he agreed. "A determined thief is hard to stop."

"The cases are heavy and have good

locks," Carol went on. "But last night the intruder had no trouble forcing them, though Mr. Kulas claims they missed the most valuable things."

The captain gave her a knowing look. "Yet they could have taken what was most valuable and negotiable for them."

The possibility of this startled her. She stared at him in surprise, wondering why he was so deeply interested in her employer's art treasures. "You could be right."

He offered her another of his charming smiles. "Well, it's really of no importance to me," he said. "Let me show you the beauty of this coastline, since this will be the last afternoon you'll have free from the hospital for a while."

And he did. They covered a considerable distance before heading back to the hotel in time for dinner. He helped Carol up onto the dock and insisted on driving her back to the Mic-Mac in the battered station wagon he had rented. She thanked him as they parted and felt it had been a thoroughly enjoyable experience.

Arthur Kulas had news for her at dinner. The diplomat told her, "I'm doing my first show tomorrow night. Mimi Gamal's aunt has to leave in a few days, and she's eager to see my presentation. The hotel has already advertised it."

"I'm looking forward to it," Carol said.

He frowned. "Of course I will have to eliminate a few numbers because of the theft. But I'll fill in with some other things."

"You should really ask the police to come by to make sure no one tries to take anything else," she suggested.

"I've thought of that," Arthur Kulas said. "I called the Mounted Police office today and requested that an officer be on hand. I also mentioned your theory about the timing of the theft. I must say they didn't seem too interested."

"I suppose they have too many other matters to look after."

"I have an important stake in this community," her employer said with some indignation. "I'm a principal shareholder of this hotel, and I deserve special consideration and protection."

"They'll undoubtedly do their best," she cajoled him.

The retired diplomat's ascetic face registered annoyance. "Their best will probably be totally unsatisfactory," he said. "And with all my preparations, you'll be leaving me tomorrow afternoon to go to that hospital."

She smiled apologetically. "I hadn't

planned it that way."

"Still, that's how it works out."

"But you've done the show so many times before," she said. "I'm sure you'll have no trouble setting it up."

"In other years I've not experienced robbery threats," he said. "Timothy Ryan has promised me two bellboys to help at the Casino, but I daren't unpack the really valuable items until just before the show."

"I'll be with you then," she reminded him. "I'll leave the hospital at six."

The prim diplomat looked somewhat placated. "That will be helpful," he said grudgingly, "though with the Kerr lad recovering, I can't think why you're so badly needed over there."

"Dr. Shaw has a lot of other patients," she told him. "The hospital is short of help."

"Well, I'll let you do as your conscience dictates," her patient said stiffly. "But I would appreciate some extra help from you tomorrow night when I do my show."

She smiled. "Don't worry about that. I want to be there. I've been looking forward to it."

This seemed to cheer him up. Later, in the lobby, she saw the printed poster announcing "Caravans and Costumes" as presented by Arthur Kulas. And standing near the sign in the brightly lighted lobby were Mimi Gamal and Walter Pitt.

Mimi Gamal was wearing one of the tight-fitting white gowns of which she seemed to have an endless supply and looking properly glamorous, while Walter Pitt, at her side, wore a white dinner jacket. Carol judged he must have come over from his own hotel to have dinner with the dusky Mimi.

Neither of them saw her as she hurriedly crossed to the elevator, an angry flush on her pretty face. She was annoyed that she should feel jealous of the debonair and carefree young man from Boston, but she did! No need to lie to herself.

Reaching her room, she sat down with a book and tried to put him out of her mind. But visions of him with Mimi kept coming back to her.

As it approached ten, she put her book aside and went downstairs. She saw Arthur Kulas playing bridge with Colonel Hooper and his wife and Mimi Gamal's aunt. Not wanting to attract their attention, she hurried to the outside lobby where Timothy Ryan was stationed by his desk.

The chubby little man said, "You've heard the news? Mr. Kulas is doing his show tomorrow night."

She nodded. "I'm looking forward to it."

"I'm not," the assistant hotel manager said glumly. "It means a lot of extra bother, and he's never satisfied with anything."

Carol smiled. "The guests should enjoy it."

"I'm thinking about myself," Timothy Ryan said dolefully. "He's already tied up two of my bellboys for the entire afternoon and evening. And that's only the beginning. You don't know him."

She left the little man still complaining and went out on the verandah to wait for Dr. Shaw. It was a bright moonlit night and not too cold.

At exactly a quarter past ten he drove up, and she hurried down and got into the front seat of the black sedan beside him. She smiled at him in the subdued light of the car's interior as they drove away from the hotel.

"I'm glad you came," she said.

He flashed her a smile from the wheel. "I said I would. I always try to keep my word. The usual business. A late accident case at the hospital. One of the farmers on the main highway got a bit too careless with his axe. Gave his foot a nasty whack, but it's all right now."

"St. Andrews should have another doctor."

"I agree. But where to find one? There's a shortage, you know."

She sat back with a sigh. "It isn't fair to you."

He smiled as he stared straight ahead at the road. "We'll not worry about it any more. We have the rest of the evening to ourselves."

"A lovely thought," she said happily.

They parked on a wharf overlooking the bay. The moonlight on the smooth water made a magic sight. She found it hard to imagine that the same bay could often be rough and treacherous. Bill talked to her about the hospital and his practice, and she told him of her experiences as a private duty nurse in Boston.

At last he said, "I'm glad you decided to come down here, that we met."

Her eyes met his, and there was a happy sparkle in them. "So am I," she said quietly.

His handsome face took on a more earnest expression. "The way you helped as scrub nurse yesterday when we operated on the Kerr lad, there was something special about you. We made a good team, Carol."

She lowered her eyes. "Thanks," she said softly.

"I don't think it should be broken up," he went on, and his arm circled her. At the same instant his lips came down on hers with a firm but gentle pressure.

When they parted she whispered, "Please, Bill, let's not try to rush things."

He studied her with concern on his handsome face. "Of course there has to be someone else."

"Not really," she said. "It's just that this is a mixed-up summer for me. I need time."

"I shouldn't let you sell me on that," he said with a wry smile, "but I will. Of course I want you to be sure. Maybe working at the hospital will help you make up your mind. I mean about the town and me."

"Perhaps it will," she agreed.

"At least you know how I feel," he said.

Carol offered him a roguish smile. "Surely I'm not the only girl you've noticed this summer. What about the glamorous Mimi Gamal?"

He shrugged. "She was my patient."

"Aside from that?" Her head was slightly to one side as she questioned him.

Bill looked embarrasssed. "What do you want me to say? She's a lovely gal, no mistake about that. It would be hard not to notice."

She quickly raised a hand. "That's enough. You don't have to tell me more. You're just another of her conquests, like all the rest of the males around here. There's a line of strewn bodies in her wake."

He laughed. "It's not that bad. She's really hardly my type. Why did you ask about her anyhow?"

"I have a theory," Carol told him. "I think she could be the one responsible for the robbery last night, or at least an accomplice." And she explained.

Bill listened. "It fits," he admitted, "depending on whether this Pitt fellow told you the truth or not. He may have been making up a story to explain being away so long."

"I've thought of that," she said. "But this time I think he told the truth."

"I doubt if you have enough grounds to make an accusation," Bill warned her. "Your best bet is to stand by and wait for more evidence."

"It could come tomorrow night. Mimi has asked Mr. Kulas to put on the show. They could try another raid on his things then."

"There's a good chance."

"Of course Walter Pitt is very friendly with Mimi," she went on unhappily. "He'll do everything he can to protect her."

Dr. Bill Shaw smiled at her knowingly. "You sound pretty interested in this Pitt."

She flounced back against the car seat. "You're wrong. He's just a crazy type I met in Boston."

"I note a certain reaction," Bill said seriously. "Maybe this is something you don't want to admit even to yourself."

"Please don't start getting Freudian and complicated," she protested. "I'm just a simple girl with simple feelings. No neuroses, no hang-ups!"

"I'd like to believe it," the young doctor chided her. He glanced at his watch. "Since we've both got big days tomorrow, it's time I took you home. Sorry I wasn't able to help you convict poor Mimi."

Carol grimaced. "You wouldn't. You're like the rest of the males — susceptible."

Bill laughed easily as he started the car and headed back to the hotel. As they drove along the main street, she saw the *Cynthia* at her wharf with lights blazing and wondered whom Captain Tim Mullaney might be entertaining at this late hour. A few minutes later they reached the front entrance of the big resort hotel.

Bill let her out, and she went directly inside. The hotel lobby was deserted. Only the sound of voices from an office at the rear broke the silence. She took the elevator to her room and went over to draw the blind before getting ready for bed. As she did so she looked out across the moonlit lawn to the Casino and saw something that made her wonder.

A strangely assorted group were standing on the steps of the entertainment building. Westy, the bass player, and his wife Jane were engaged in an earnest conversation with Mimi Gamal and her aunt. After a moment they moved down the steps to the musician's station wagon and got into it. The tall, broad-shouldered Westy gazed furtively around for a second before sliding behind the wheel of the station wagon and driving the odd company away!

CHAPTER NINE

As soon as they finished breakfast the next morning, Arthur Kulas had his several trunks taken over to the Casino building and began instructing the baffled bellhops as to how he wanted the stage decorated. While they stood by with yards of velvet drapes in hand, he lectured them on his past triumphs. Carol, seated in the front row of the small auditorium, was also a captive audience.

"The entire effect depends on the staging," he solemnly assured them. "I must have the drapes set up properly. What I'm presenting here is probably the most lavish and authentic display of Middle-Eastern costumes ever seen in America; not to mention the ancient wall hangings and Persian rugs I feature in my program."

The job took the entire morning.

Carol was impressed by the dark velvet background with the decorative stripes of gold at each end. "I think you have a wonderful stage setting," she said.

A perspiring Arthur Kulas mopped his brow as he smiled at her. "I'm glad you approve. Of course I've gone to a lot more bother here than I did when I was giving lectures in clubs every day. Then I had to make do with a much more simple setting." He eyed the decorated stage with pleasure. "But here I can sort of spread out."

The older of the two bellboys approached him cautiously. "Can we go now, sir?" he wanted to know.

"Not at all," the retired diplomat said primly. "I want you to remain here throughout the day and evening. You can work in alternate shifts, but I want someone to guard the locked trunks backstage every minute. Do you understand?"

"Yes, sir," the boy said, looking abashed.

At the same instant there was loud clapping from the darkened rear of the big room. "Bravo!" a familiar voice rang out. Carol recognized it as belonging to Colonel Bart Hooper.

The colonel and his wife came forward to join them. The diminutive Ellen clasped her hands and smiled delightedly at the stage setting. "I just can't wait to see all those lovely things, Mr. Kulas," she said in her gushing Southern fashion.

The diplomat bowed. "My pleasure to allow you to inspect them personally after the performance," he promised her.

The tiny woman smiled at the colonel. "You hear that, dear?"

The balding man with the shrewd eyes gave one of his hooting laughs. "I can hardly wait," he said. And he turned to Carol. "Are you also a part of the performance, my dear?"

"No," she said. "My duty is only to watch out that Mr. Kulas does not overdo himself."

"And a worthy one," the beak-nosed Colonel Hooper declared as he squeezed her arm and offered her a knowing smile. Then he told Arthur Kulas, "Ellen and I were hoping you might join us in some noon-time refreshments."

Ellen smiled sweetly. "We've counted on it, so don't disappoint us."

The retired diplomat gave the stage a concerned glance but then seemed to relax. He told the two, "Perhaps a rest and some good conversation would be the best thing for me."

Carol was delighted to see the three of them leave together. She had no more than enough time to get lunch, change her clothes and report at the St. Andrews hospital. She allowed them to go ahead before she left the darkened auditorium. When she finally went out to the sunlight of the verandah, who should be standing there in white tennis shorts but Walter Pitt?

The handsome young man from Boston was wearing dark glasses and smiling. He had a tennis racquet in his hand. "How about a game before lunch?" he asked.

Carol gave him an arch look. "I'm afraid not. I haven't time." And she started for the steps to the sidewalk below.

He followed her. "Come now; you can't be that busy!" he objected. "You sat around watching that old crackpot set up his stage all morning."

She gave him a reproving look over her shoulder as she started down the steps. "I'd appreciate your referring to my employer with more respect," she told him.

"Sorry," he said. "But you did just sit

around while he fussed away the entire morning."

She hesitated, her hand on the railing. "Were you watching?"

The tanned young man looked embarrassed. "I'm never far away from you."

"I wish I could say that cheered me," she told him. "But it doesn't."

He gazed at her imploringly. "You really aren't fair to me, you know. It's because we got off to a bad start at our first meeting. If you'd only try to forget that!"

"Please!" she said, still hesitating midway down the steps. "I haven't time to listen to the entire history of our acquaintance, and I'm sure Miss Gamal can give you all the attention you seem to need so badly."

"She's just a girl!" he said despairingly. "You're something special to me. I wish you'd believe that."

Carol met his gaze. "Mr. Pitt," she said sweetly, "until the age of twelve I was extremely fond of fairy tales and believed in them implicitly. Since then I've inclined to a mere realistic outlook! Please excuse me!" And she hurried on down the steps and toward the towering old-English style hotel building.

"Carol!" Walter Pitt called after her unhappily. But he didn't attempt to follow her.

A smile played on her pretty face as she entered the hotel lobby. As she hurried to the elevator she abruptly came face to face with the glamorous Lebanese, and had to halt quickly to avoid bumping into her.

"Miss Holly," Mimi said in her accented voice, "how nice to see you!"

"Nice to see you," Carol said breathlessly. "I'm in a hurry, but I didn't mean to run you down."

Mimi gave her a sultry look of amusement. "Poor Miss Holly! Always so serious and always in such a hurry! Do you manage to get any fun out of life at all?"

"I'm not exactly a jet set princess," Carol said grimly. "But I manage."

Mimi threw back her head and revealed pearly white teeth as she laughed. "You have a sense of humor!" she said. "That is good!"

Carol decided since she'd been delayed, she might as well make the most of her time. With an expression of studied innocence, she asked, "Did you enjoy your midnight motor ride with Westy and his wife?"

At once the dark girl looked serious. "I do not know what you mean."

"I saw you and your aunt getting into the station wagon with Westy and his wife at the Casino last night. I looked out of my window. It must have been after midnight."

Mimi Gamal had regained her poise. She smiled. "I fear you must have made an error, Miss Holly. My aunt is never out past nine, and I was not at the Casino last night, though I do intend to go there for the lecture of Mr. Kulas this evening, and so does my aunt. Poor dear, she is leaving tomorrow."

"So I understand," Carol said coolly. "I hope she enjoys the show. If you'll excuse me, I'm in a hurry." And she moved on to the open elevator without waiting for a reply from the dark girl.

A host of questions continued to plague her, but she forced them out of her mind as she rushed to get to the hospital in time. A hurried lunch and a short drive in the station wagon, which Arthur Kulas had kindly offered to let her use, brought her to St. Andrews hospital. Bill Shaw was waiting in his office to greet her.

He rose from behind his desk as he surveyed her in her crisp white uniform and cap. "A sight for weary eyes," he said with a smile, as he came around the desk to join her. "I hope I didn't keep you out too late last night."

She shook her head. "It was a wonderful evening."

His eyes twinkled. "I rather fancied it myself." He sighed. "And now it's down to business. I'm afraid the first thing I'm going to ask you to do is change into the drab outfit of a scrub nurse and assist me in an open fracture reduction. A young man smashed himself up nicely on a motorcycle on the St. Stephen highway about a half-hour ago. He's waiting for surgery now."

Carol showed concern. "How bad is it?"

"Fortunately, the main damage is confined to his left leg," Bill said. "He has multiple fractures that must be attended to at once. He'll probably require traction when we've finished with him. He'll be lucky if we're able to save the leg. It's a mess!"

She gave a small shiver. "I hate motor-cycles."

"I'm not a hundred percent for them," he agreed.

"How is Andy Kerr's son making out?"

"Very well." He smiled. "You'll see him after the operation. I'll take you on a round of the patients then."

She followed him to the rear of the building where the modest operating room was located. In the scrub room, she found Nurse Caine already on hand and waiting to serve as circulating nurse.

The stout woman beamed at her through

her horn-rimmed glasses. "Give Dr. Shaw credit," she said. "He hasn't wasted any time making use of your abilities."

And it was only too true. Before she realized what was happening, Carol stood by the operating table in green cap, mask and gown. A gowned and masked Dr. Bill Shaw stood across the stainless steel table from her as orderlies brought in the young man patient. Nurse Caine was doubling as anesthetist in the short-staffed hospital.

The young man was already drowsy from earlier oral anesthesia, and his eyes were closed. His face was waxen, and Nurse Caine administered the main anesthesia with some caution. Dr. Bill Shaw watched carefully, noting the patient's heartbeat and respiratory action.

When the white sheet was turned back to reveal the twisted, bleeding leg, Carol had a moment of revulsion. Then she answered Dr. Bill Shaw's sharp command for instruments, and the operation was under way. The young doctor worked quickly, and his skilled slim hands manipulated the broken bones into place once the flesh had been turned back. Bringing the fragmented ends of the lower leg bone together, he inserted metal screws that would hold them in place until the bones healed properly. The screws could also remain there for the life of the patient. Afterward, when all the bone damage had been repaired, a cast was applied to the injured leg.

Carol knew from experience it would mean a hospital stay of at least ten days for the accident victim. And it could well mean another nine months of immobilization until his full recovery a year or so hence. A high price to pay for an afternoon's fun. But he would walk again, and probably without a trace of a limp. That was the hopeful thought in her mind as the patient was wheeled out.

Dr. Shaw whipped off his mask with a smile. "I'm glad you were here for that one," he said. "If I'd had only Nurse Caine, I'd have had to send him on to St. Stephen. And it's better for him here, since this is his home."

Carol gave a relieved sigh. "I'm glad it's over. I'd hardly gotten my breath before you had me in here."

"The pace will be less hectic for the rest of the afternoon," the young doctor promised. "When you've changed, I'll take you around to meet the rest of the staff and the patients."

Carol found this a pleasant and relaxing experience. And since the hospital was a small one, it didn't take too long. They first visited the private room where Andy Kerr's son was recuperating from his brain injuries. The orchestra leader was sitting by his son's bedside when they entered and got up to greet them.

"Hear you had another motorcycle accident victim today," the pudgy musician said with a serious expression on his owl-like face. "There should be a law against them."

"I'm almost ready to agree," Bill said. "How's the boy?"

Andy glanced toward the bed where his son grinned wanly from his pillow. "First rate," he declared, "but still weak. However, that's to be expected."

"It is," Bill agreed. And he went over to examine the boy, leaving Carol standing with the musician.

Andy Kerr smiled at her. "I'm not forgetting you helped save my lad's life," he declared. "And I'm also grateful to be getting the night off tonight because of the lecture Mr. Kulas will be giving."

"I hadn't thought about that. It will mean a free evening for you."

"That it will," the orchestra leader agreed.

She decided to ask him about the mysterious Westy. "How long will Westy be playing with you?" she asked.

The stout little man frowned. "I can't say. He's a strange one. Knows how to handle a bass, no question of that. But there's something about him I don't take to. And he doesn't seem really interested in the job."

"I have the same impression," she said. "Have you ever been out to his place?"

"No. He keeps to himself, him and that wife of his," Andy said with a scowl. "They're not friendly."

"I think they are friends of two of the hotel guests," Carol said. "I've seen them with Mimi Gamal and her aunt."

"You mean the dark pin-up gal?"

She smiled. "That's the one."

Andy looked blank. "First I knew of it. How would they get to know each other?"

"That's what I've been wondering," Carol said.

Before she had a chance to pursue the subject further, Dr. Shaw returned to touch a hand gently to her elbow. "It's time we were moving on. I'll show you the other private-room patients first."

Their next stop was at the room of one of the summer visitors who had come down with a serious gallstone attack during the early summer season. Dr. Bill Shaw had operated on the pleasant matron, and she was now well on the way to recovery.

Before they entered the room, Bill Shaw told Carol, "She's a charming person, but not too serious-minded. I don't object, except that she insists on a lot of extra attention and service. She and her husband own one of the largest summer homes here. Her name is Mrs. Anderson."

The henna-haired Mrs. Anderson was sitting bolstered against several pillows, watching a portable television set at the foot of her bed, when they went into her room. She flicked the set off with a remote control switch which she manipulated from her bed.

"I'm glad you came, Doctor," she said brightly. "I get so sick of these television shows."

"I wanted you to meet an addition to our staff," Bill Shaw said. And he introduced Carol.

"Well, I'm glad to meet you, Nurse Holly," Mrs. Anderson said in her happy way. "Thank goodness Dr. Shaw has seen me almost all the way through this ordeal. I do hope to have some parties before the season is over. You must come to one of them."

Bill Shaw lifted a reproving finger. "Let's not start thinking about parties so soon," he told the wealthy woman.

Mrs. Anderson pouted. "But I do want to

155

have some fun before the season ends. And you said I'd be out of the hospital next week."

"You'll have to take it very easy at first," the young doctor warned her.

"I will," Mrs. Anderson assured him. "I'll let Timothy Ryan and the hotel catering staff look after everything. Surely then you can't object to my having a few friends in?"

Bill laughed. "I suppose not."

As they left the society matron, she beamed at Carol. "So nice to have met you, Nurse Holly," she said.

In the corridor, Bill Shaw told Carol confidentially, "In spite of her interest in having fun, she's really a rather wonderful, sincere person. And she's good-natured, which I can't say for the next patient you're going to meet."

Carol opened her eyes wide. "You make it sound as if you're going to introduce me to some kind of ogre."

Bill chuckled. As they neared the next door, he told her in a low tone, "This is a patient I'd like to send home. But he does need strict medical attention. He has a serious ulcer condition. It's Donald Winter, the famous novelist. He's done a lot of books about Ireland and St. Andrews."

Donald Winter had been resting, with his

eyes closed. As they came in, he rose up in bed and gave them a wary glance. He was a rather good-looking man late middle age, with fine features, graying hair and the general air of a hard-drinking cynic.

He said, "Well?"

Bill Shaw told him, "I wanted you to meet Nurse Holly."

The novelist's face lit up with an interested smile as he took Carol's hand and held it. "Welcome to the charnel house, Miss Holly. You're a welcome addition."

"Thank you," she said.

Bill Shaw cleared his throat. "Miss Holly came here as private nurse for Arthur Kulas. But he's been kind enough to lend her to the hospital for part of each day."

"Has he now?" The novelist smiled, still staring up at her, "Well, old Arthur always did have good taste, even if he is the world's worst bore! He must be getting dotty as well in his old age to part with a gem like you for even a few hours."

Carol blushed, wishing the novelist would free her hand. "He's not so ill that he requires a full-time private nurse," she said.

"The old fraud is not ill at all," Donald Winter said grandly. "He's had diabetes for years. Now I'm really afflicted. Dr. Shaw hasn't allowed me a drink since I've been in here."

Bill smiled. "There is always a pitcher of water at your bedside."

"Water!" the man in bed said with disgust. But he did finally release Carol's hand.

When they left his room a moment afterward, Carol laughed and said, "It's too bad Mr. Winter hasn't met Mimi Gamal."

"Don't mention her!" Dr. Shaw implored her. "First thing you know, he'd be sneaking out of the hospital."

The other private patient was one of the wealthy owners of estates in the resort town; her name was Muriel Capper. She had a weight problem and had suffered a mild heart attack from which she was recovering. She eyed Carol in a friendly fashion.

"Arthur Kulas and I have known each other for years," she said. "He and my late husband were friends. I used to play the piano when he visited our apartment in Boston."

"Mrs. Capper is a talented pianist and an artist as well," Bill Shaw informed Carol.

"Music came naturally to me, and the nuns taught me art," Mrs. Capper said proudly. "I was educated in a private school operated by the Sisters of Charity. Where did you receive your education, Miss Holly?"

"In Boston," Carol said.

"We must talk about it," the stout woman said dolefully. "And calories. We must discuss calories a lot. There are so many theories, you know. And I'm afraid they've been my downfall."

Dr. Shaw gave Carol an amused glance when they left Mrs. Capper's room. "Well, that's the last of the plush summer crowd," he said. "Now we'll visit the wards and the really sick people."

Carol spent the remainder of the afternoon attending to the needs of the various wards. And when six o'clock arrived she was exhausted.

Dr. Bill Shaw had already left to go on some house calls, and only Nurse Caine was there to see her off. The stout nurse gave her a grateful look. "We've been able to keep the patients a lot more comfortable, thanks to your being here today," she said.

"I enjoyed being here," Carol replied, "though I'm afraid I didn't do much to make Donald Winter happy."

Nurse Caine rolled her eyes in resignation. "Don't worry about him!"

Carol drove quickly back to the hotel. On impulse she stopped first by the Casino to find out if Arthur Kulas might be there making additional changes in the stage setting. But when she stood at the back of the dark auditorium she saw that it was deserted. Then she was startled by a rustling noise backstage.

CHAPTER TEN

Carol stood completely still, listening, and the sound of movement from backstage came again. It occurred to her that it might be Arthur Kulas, so she went down the aisle and backstage. But it wasn't her employer she discovered bending over one of the heavy metal trunks in the eerie shadows, but Walter Pitt!

The young man from Boston was in dark slacks and a brown shirt open at the neck. He glanced up at her with a look of uneasiness. "Well," he said, "I didn't expect to find you here!"

"And I certainly didn't expect to find you here!" she said acidly. "What are you doing prying into my employer's things?"

He got up placatingly. "Now don't get all fussed up about nothing," he said.

"About nothing?" she demanded.

He spread his hands and looked innocent. "I simply came backstage because I was interested. I've heard so much about the lecture."

"You have no right to be here!" she said sternly. "There is supposed to be a bellboy standing guard over the precious items in these trunks."

The young man glanced around. "Well, I certainly don't see anyone. Do you?"

"That doesn't mean he shouldn't be here," she said sternly. "I'll ask you to leave. And I'm going to tell Mr. Kulas about finding you here."

"You're not very friendly," Walter Pitt observed.

"And I don't consider you very discreet," was Carol's reply. "Please get out of here."

He did so reluctantly. And she followed to make sure he left the building. When they reached the sidewalk outside the Casino, he gave her a pleading glance. "I hope you're not going to hold this against me."

"I'll let Mr. Kulas deal with you," she said as she left him to head for the hotel.

She informed her employer of her discovery while she was giving him his medication in his suite before going downstairs to dinner. His reaction was not what she'd expected. In fact, he embarked on a series of surprisingly impractical moves.

"Where were the bellboys?" he demanded

indignantly. "Timothy Ryan will have some explaining to do."

As soon as they went downstairs, he tackled the chubby Timothy Ryan in the lobby. "Do you realize those young rascals aren't guarding my show?" he demanded of the harassed little man.

Timothy Ryan ran a finger inside his collar while perspiration gleamed at his temples. "I had to call on them, Mr. Kulas. I needed extra help for the cocktail hour."

"And so many valuables were left open to robbers," Arthur Kulas said angrily. "The hotel's board of directors will hear about this." And without mentioning Pitt, he stamped off in the direction of the dining room with Carol at his heels.

When dinner was over, she accompanied him into the inner lobby where Mimi Gamal and her aunt, in evening gowns, greeted him effusively. "We are looking forward so much to your lecture," the dusky Mimi gushed.

Carol went backstage with him at the Casino, where he complained of a headache. She brought him some aspirin and advised him to remain as calm as possible, which advice he accepted with undisguised annoyance.

"I'm not a simpleton, Miss Holly, so

kindly do not treat me like one," he told her as he downed the aspirin and some water. Handing back the glass, he asked, "Do I look presentable?"

"You look very well," Carol said sincerely. He was wearing a dark crimson dinner jacket with black trousers and tie. His graying hair gave him just the right touch of distinction, and though his classic features were pale, it did not detract from his general appearance.

"I hope you enjoy the show," he said, glancing at his wristwatch. "Take a look and see if the audience has assembled."

She went to the side of the stage and peered out through a slit in the curtains. The auditorium was indeed full, with Colonel Hooper and his wife Ellen sitting in the front row with smiles on their faces. Farther back in the group she spotted Mimi Gamal and her aunt, with Captain Tim Mullaney sitting beside them. Carol strained to catch a glimpse of Walter Pitt somewhere in the rows of spectators but didn't see him. And of course Dr. Bill Shaw had been much too busy to consider attending.

She went back to her employer. "Every seat seems to be filled," she said.

"Then that's the time to begin," Arthur Kulas told her. "Nothing to be gained by keeping them waiting." And buttoning the single button of his crimson jacket, he marched onstage.

There was a mild scattering of applause. Then he began, saying, "Let us take an imaginary journey through the Middle East. It's not entirely imaginary, since along the way you shall be shown silks and satins, linen and brocades, carpets and tapestries the like of which you have never encountered before!"

From where she stood in the wings, Carol had an excellent view of the combined lecture and show. Arthur Kulas quickly changed from exotic costume to exotic costume with a dexterity which belied his age and general health.

And the audience was responding. There was laughter in the right places and continuous rounds of applause. As she watched, Carol could understand why the presentations had come to mean so much to the retired diplomat. There was something definitely creative about the lecture, and it seemed to her that Arthur Kulas had brought forth an art form peculiar to himself.

The lecture lasted sixty minutes without an intermission, and when it ended there was a burst of enthusiastic clapping. Arthur

Kulas came off the stage in an especially colorful Arabian robe and headdress.

His face was flushed and happy as he asked her. "Was it a success?"

"Simply wonderful," she assured him.

"I feel a trifle weary," he confessed. "But I'm glad it went well." Before he could say any more, a horde of fans came backstage to surround him, including the curvaceous, dark-skinned Mimi Gamal.

"We have a party planned for you at the lake," the Lebanese girl told him.

Arthur Kulas looked surprised. "A party? I really don't feel up to it."

"But my aunt is leaving tomorrow," she protested. "And we shall not keep you long. Westy and his wife have made all the preparations. It was to be a surprise."

Carol, who had been standing close by, heard the dark girl. And now she understood why she'd seen her and her aunt with Westy and Jane.

Arthur Kulas turned to Carol. "What do you think, Miss Holly?"

"You've had a very hard day," she reminded him. "And there are your things to be put away."

"I could pack them quickly if that dolt of a Timothy Ryan would assign a watchman to guard them," the retired diplomat said testily.

"By all means let us help," Mimi Gamal suggested.

The hard-faced Westy and his wife, who were also in the group backstage, joined in with offers to assist. They at once began to pack the things away.

When the last trunk had been locked, Arthur Kulas stood up and said, "We can join the party now, but only for a short time. And Miss Holly must come along. I'm not feeling up to par."

Mimi Gamal smiled, showing her pearly teeth. "But naturally Miss Holly is invited," she said.

Westy, standing by with a grin on his big square face, nodded. "We wouldn't think of leaving you out of this, baby."

Carol ignored the remark.

They all bundled into Westy's station wagon and began the somewhat bumpy journey out to the isolated house by Chamcook Lake. Carol had heard it described as big, rambling and spooky. But it was supposed to have a wonderful location on the very edge of the lake which supplied water to St. Andrews.

At last the station wagon came to halt on a small rise overlooking the lake. Just beside them stood the old summerhouse, darkly outlined and ominous in the silent summer night.

Westy turned off the engine. "We've arrived," he said cheerily. "All out!"

Arthur Kulas groaned. "I'm not sure I'll be able to walk. I'm dizzy and nauseated!"

Carol assisted the tottering ex-diplomat out of the station wagon, and they followed the others in the direction of the summerhouse. Lights went on, and they could see the steps leading to a verandah overlooking the lake and the front entrance of the old house.

Arthur Kulas hesitated for a moment, taking in the surroundings. He peered out at the lake, ghostly now in the dark night. "It is a beautiful location," he admitted, "but much too difficult to get to."

Westy was right behind them. "You'll have plenty of time to rest before you make the return trip," the big, broad-shouldered bass player said. "I'm real honored to have you as a guest, Mr. Kulas."

Carol's employer regarded the big man grimly. "I trust you realize it has almost wrecked my health to be here. Please lead the way."

The big man did, and a few minutes later they were seated on a divan in a big gloomy living room. Jane, busy supplying everyone with drinks, finally came to Carol and Arthur Kulas.

"What would you like?" the hard-faced woman asked the ex-diplomat.

"Sherry, if you have a good brand," the classic-faced man replied. And Carol said she would have the same.

Gradually two things became noticeable to her. One, they were seated on the divan at one end of the room with all the others grouped facing them and between them and the exit. Two, Mimi Gamal had paid no attention to Arthur Kulas at all, now that he'd accepted her invitation to the party. The pretty dark girl continued to gabble with her aunt in their native tongue. This was not in character. Carol studied the group uneasily and began to feel nervous.

Jane brought them the sherries with a grim smile on her face. "You two want to enjoy yourselves. You're the guests of honor, after all."

Mimi, across from them and seated on the arm of an easy chair in which her aunt reclined, laughed suddenly and harshly. "Yes, the guests of honor," she repeated in a tone which definitely was not humorous. In fact, Carol considered it menacing.

Come to think of it, there was an air of

threatening violence in the whole atmosphere of the big gloomy room. She looked at Arthur Kulas to see if he'd become conscious of it. It took only a glance to know that he had.

His sherry untouched, the ex-diplomat asked, "Just what is going on here?"

Westy came forward to stand facing him, only a few feet away. A nasty grin spread across his square face. "Why, this is a party, Mr. Kulas. What else?"

"I don't like your tone!" Arthur Kulas sputtered, and jumped up.

"Take it easy, mister," Westy said in an ugly voice, and at the same instant shoved the slim man in the crimson dinner jacket back down on the divan beside Carol.

The sherry in his glass was spilled, and the diplomat's jaw sagged with consternation. "How dare you treat me this way?"

Mimi Gamal had come forward to stand by Westy.

"We will dare a lot to get what we want, Mr. Kulas," she said evenly.

The diplomat frowned. "Get what you want? Are you insane? I don't know what all this means."

Jane had come to take her place in the line-up. "Don't try to be funny, Kulas," she said. "You remember Sousa."

"Sousa!" The diplomat repeated the name in a startled voice. "What has he to do with this? He's in an Egyptian jail, poor devil! I haven't seen him in years."

The burly Westy became more angry and roughly grasped the ex-diplomat by the shirt front. The beefy face of the bass player showed sheer hatred. "All right, Mister Kulas," he grated. "We've played long enough. You know what we're after — the treasure that Sousa stole from that tomb. He gave you the map. Where is it?"

"What map?" Arthur Kulas blinked up at him in bewilderment.

"Let him alone!" Carol cried, and rose to break the big man's hold on her employer.

But Mimi Gamal quickly intruded to grapple with her and draw her back. She was joined by Jane, and between them the two women held Carol away from the diplomat.

Mimi's lip curled. "You will behave now," she said, still grasping Carol's arm.

Carol vainly twisted to free herself from the grip of the two, but it was useless. She cried, "You'll answer to the police for this, you know!"

Westy turned to her with a nasty grin on his big flat face. "Don't try to interfere in this. It's a family matter. Mimi's a thirty-second cousin of Sousa, and she's entitled to the treasure!"

"I don't know anything about what Sousa took from the tomb," a tense Arthur Kulas insisted. "All I have are the art items I use in the show."

Westy looked disgusted. "That stuff!" he said with impatience. "It's nothing compared to what Sousa's got hidden away. And we know you have the map, because he says so."

"It's not true!" the disheveled diplomat protested. He glanced fearfully in Carol's direction. "And make those hussies release my nurse."

"All in good time," Westy said in an easy tone, a big fist clenched and held above Arthur Kulas. "Now I'm going to let you have just a minute or two to remember, and then I'm giving you the treatment."

The ex-diplomat gazed apprehensively at the fist hovering above him. "No!"

"Where's the map?" Westy asked menacingly. "That's all we need to know; then you can go free!"

"I'd tell you if I could," the man on the divan said. "I honestly don't know. And certainly Miss Holly should not be involved in this!"

"Miss Holly is involved," Westy assured

him. "The girls can make it rough for her if we have to get you to talk."

Arthur Kulas glanced over at the lovely Mimi with loathing. "And to think I let you trick me into this."

"Be sensible," the dark girl advised him. "We've waited long enough. Westy has a nasty temper."

"Scum, all of you!" the ex-diplomat cried angrily.

"Okay, Kulas," Westy said. "You've asked for it." And he swung his clenched fist to catch the fragile Arthur Kulas full in the face. Blood spurted from the diplomat's lips, and he tumbled back on the divan.

"Not too rough, Westy," the big man's wife warned. "You want him to be able to talk."

"He'll be able to talk," Westy said, grasping the stricken Kulas by the shirt front again and raising him up. But the ex-diplomat was white-faced and seemingly near unconsciousness.

"He's ill!" Carol shouted. "You'll kill him!" But there seemed little hope her warning would be heeded.

Then she heard a sound, and knew it was an approaching car. The roar of its motor came nearer, and now Westy heard it as well. The big man let Arthur Kulas drop back on the divan a second time and turned with a frightened expression on his beefy face. His hand went quickly to a rear pocket, and he drew out a shining automatic.

Carol decided to try to scare the bass player. "It's the police!" she cried. "I was suspicious of you inviting us out here, and I asked them to make a check."

Mimi Gamal looked frightened. She glanced from Carol to the big man. "You think she's telling the truth?"

The automatic glistened in his hand as he crouched there, listening to the approaching car. "I don't know," he said.

Jane's face showed fear. "We can't take a chance!"

Mimi Gamal slackened her hold on Carol slightly. "She's right! It could be the police! He's had them around!" The ugly aunt was on her feet and also looking agitated as Westy continued to hesitate.

"We'll take the boat!" he announced finally.

Carol suddenly realized she was not being held as tightly as before and took the opportunity to break free of the two women and make for the door. As she did so, she heard Westy shout out a warning to her. She heard the report of a gun and felt the heat of a bullet finding its mark in her skull. With a dull moan she collapsed. . . .

When she opened her eyes, Carol was looking up into the friendly red-bearded face of Captain Tim Mullaney. The big Irishman said softly, "It's all right, my colleen. The bullet just barely grazed your head. You're going to live and maybe win a beauty contest."

She stared up at him in bewilderment. "Where are Westy and the others?"

The big man grinned cynically. "They left in the power boat just as we arrived. By this time they're somewhere on the other side of the lake. No doubt they've got a car waiting there to make their getaway."

"Oh, no!" she protested.

"That kind of rogues have the nine lives of a cat," Mullaney assured her. "Do you feel well enough to sit up?"

"I think so," she said. "How is Mr. Kulas?"

"Aside from losing a couple of teeth, your patient is in excellent shape," the bearded captain said jokingly.

Carol sat up and saw her employer seated on the divan, holding his head in his hands in a dejected manner. She gazed at the jovial captain again. "You got here just in time," she told him. "How did you know we were here?"

Before he could make any reply, someone else entered the room. She turned to see who it was and gave a tiny gasp. It was the young man from Boston, Walter Pitt!

"You!" she said.

He nodded with a wry grin. "Me. You ought to be glad to see me this time."

She swallowed hard and glanced from the grinning captain kneeling at her side to the young man standing in the middle of the room. "Were you two together?"

Walter Pitt nodded. "Yes. We heard about the party and decided to try and crash it."

"Oh, no!" Carol said despairingly.

Captain Tim Mullaney chuckled. "Admittedly our motive was ignoble, but we did manage to accomplish an heroic feat. Of such bungling is history made."

"With you mixed up in it, I might have know it was just an accident," Carol said woefully to Walter. "I suppose they got away."

"I'm afraid so," the young man from Boston admitted. "It's a wide lake with a road on the other side leading back to the highway. Unless we get to the police right away, we haven't a chance to catch them."

"Isn't there a phone here?" she wailed.

"No. They even have their own lighting plant," the captain said. "Our best bet is to load up in my station wagon and get back to the main road and the nearest phone as quickly as possible."

"Come along," Walter Pitt said, reaching down to assist Carol to her feet.

Carol stood shakily with the young man's arm around her. She gave him a dismal look. "I'm only allowing you to hold me because I'm so weak," she told him.

Walter Pitt smiled. "I realize that."

"Will he be all right?" she asked, indicating Arthur Kulas.

Captain Tim Mullaney nodded. "Don't worry your pretty bullet-singed head," he said in his Irish brogue. "I'll take care of him."

So, a few minutes later, Carol found herself in the Irishman's station wagon, beside Walter Pitt in the rear seat. Her employer shared the front seat with the captain and groaned as they began the rough journey back to the main road. Carol gave a small sigh as she nestled close to the man at her side, grateful for the comfort of his arm around her. For once the young man from Boston was welcome!

CHAPTER ELEVEN

Arthur Kulas sat dejectedly on the divan in his suite as he gave the details of the evening's happenings to the Mounted Police officer. Dr. Bill Shaw had come to attend to both Carol and the ex-diplomat's injuries and then been called away by an emergency. Walter Pitt and the genial captain still remained in the suite helping fill in details as required. Carol, with some of her hair clipped away and the graze covered by an adhesive bandage, sat close to her employer listening to him.

Arthur Kulas had a patch of tape near his mouth, and his lips were swollen. Otherwise he looked much like his normal self. "I simply can't understand it," he exclaimed for perhaps the tenth time. "That Gamal girl seemed such a perfect lady."

The Mounted Police officer, who was standing in the middle of the room in khaki uniform as he solemnly took notes, gave the older man an understanding glance. "I'm afraid this is usually the case, sir. Criminals of her class are difficult to spot."

"Criminals!" the ex-diplomat exclaimed. "I think you should be most careful about branding the young lady in that manner.

And her aunt was surely a modest, retiring woman."

The young officer paused in taking his notes. "I'm sorry, but the evidence is all against them, sir. Otherwise they wouldn't have run off as they did."

Her employer frowned at the carpet. "I suppose you're right. It's enough to make a person lose all faith in human nature." He looked in the direction of Walter Pitt and the red-bearded captain. "But I must say I owe a huge debt to you two."

"Sure, we were only too happy to be of service," Tim Mullaney said in his thick brogue.

"We deserve no credit," Walter Pitt said again. "We planned to try crashing the party."

"And a good thing you did," Arthur Kulas said emphatically. "You saved us from goodness knows what! I take it you were both to my lecture."

The captain and Walter Pitt exchanged knowing glances. And then Tim Mullaney said, "That we were. And a lovely treat it was. Sure everyone enjoyed it."

Her employer at once looked happier. "I'm glad you enjoyed it. I pride myself that it is unique in America." And he sat up proudly.

The police officer cleared his throat. "One thing, Mr. Kulas. These references to a Mr. Sousa and a map — do they mean anything to you?"

The ex-diplomat's ascetic face took on a frown. "No, they don't. I can't imagine what that brute Westy was talking about. Of course I did know Sousa."

"Who was he?" the officer asked curtly.

Arthur Kulas made a small gesture with his right hand. "A man who was hired to look after the contracting for the excavation of an ancient tomb. As it turned out, he wasn't honest. Stole a good deal of the treasure for himself. Too bad! Otherwise he was a very pleasant chap. But you know, still water and all that."

"He gave you some sort of map," the young officer persisted.

Her employer looked indignant. "There you are wrong! He didn't! Not at any time did I receive a map from Sousa."

"This Westy claimed you did," the mounted policeman pointed out.

"I know." Arthur Kulas sighed. "And I can't think why, unless the fellow is mad. Sousa was in jail when I left Egypt."

"So you claim you know nothing about a map," the officer said.

"I do know nothing about one," the fragile

man said with a hint of anger. "Really, I think you should be trying to locate those people instead of giving me the third degree."

"There are certain facts I had to find out," the young officer said. "And you can be assured an alarm has gone out for the criminals on both sides of the border."

"Well, I should certainly think so," a disgruntled Arthur Kulas said. "There are such things as law and order. You have witnessed what they did to me and my nurse, Miss Holly."

The Mounted Policeman smiled at Carol. "I'm quite aware of it, sir," he said.

Carol took the opportunity of asking the officer, "Will you need me any longer?"

"I think not," he said.

She got up and turned to her employer. "Then if you feel you'll be all right, Mr. Kulas, I believe I'll go to bed. It's been a very long day."

"By all means," the ex-diplomat said, rising. And he added solicitously, "I'm most sorry for all that happened."

"Please don't worry about it," she said. And she went out. She was a trifle surprised to find that Walter Pitt was following her into the corridor.

She paused and asked, "Why did you

come after me?"

The young man from Boston smiled brashly. "I suppose it's gotten to be a habit."

"It's one I'd try to break at once," she advised him.

He looked forlorn. "But you were so pleased to see me earlier."

"Under the circumstances, I'd have been pleased to see anyone," she reminded him.

"But I probably saved your life," he pointed out.

"You were trying to crash a party," she said with a thin smile. "You've already admitted that. So don't expect any medal for bravery."

"All the really brave people are over-looked," he said with a sigh. "Try and get a good sleep. No use asking you about a game of tennis in the morning."

She raised a hand to her injury. "With this head, no," she said. "I do thank you though."

The young man's face lit up. "Good night, Carol," he said. "I hope your head doesn't ache too much."

"I hope not," she echoed. She let herself into her room and closed the door after her.

She went to bed immediately. And while she had no trouble getting to sleep, since she was exhausted, she did have a problem with dreams. And in all her dreams Mimi Gamal and Westy tortured and tormented her. When she awoke with a small cry, the sun was streaming in through her window, and the phone at her bedside was ringing.

Sleepily she reached for the receiver and croaked, "Yes?"

"You sound awful!" a concerned Dr. Bill Shaw said from the other end of the line. "Are you feeling ill?"

She was more awake now and sat up with an amused expression on her pretty face. "No. I was dead asleep when the phone rang, that's all."

"I'm glad to hear that," he said with relief. "I phoned to tell you not to worry about coming in to the hospital today."

"There's no reason I shouldn't, unless Mr. Kulas needs me," she protested. "I feel perfectly all right." And then she added, "Oh, dear! I wonder how he is. I should have been in to see him before this, but I overslept."

Dr. Bill Shaw chuckled from the other end of the line. "You needn't worry. I gave him some sleeping tablets. He's overslept too. You're sure you want to come in today?"

"Positive," she said.

"I'll see you at one then," the young doctor said.

Putting down the phone, she hastily showered and dressed and then went to see how her employer was making out. True to the young doctor's prediction, he had risen late. He was in one of his irate moods and feeling extremely sorry for himself.

Striding back and forth in his dressing gown, he said indignantly, "What an ending for a wonderful evening! My lecture won the audience, you know that. And then to have that dreadful thing happen! I still can't believe that Miss Gamal would be party to such a plot."

Carol attempted to placate him. "You must try to forget it and let the police look after it," she said. "It's a lovely day. Why don't you go down and do some putting?"

"Putting!" the ex-diplomat said with disgust. "I have no time for sports this morning. We're going over to the Casino and repack those trunks and have them brought back here. Timothy Ryan was supposed to keep a night watchman there last night to guard them. But you know you can't really trust him!"

Carol did what she could to calm her difficult patient. Things weren't helped when he went downstairs. The resort hotel appeared to have been buzzing with talk of the events at Chamcook Lake, and the ex-diplomat was offered sympathy on all sides.

Colonel Hooper and Ellen were among the first to crowd close and utter their condolences.

"We were told St. Andrews was such a quiet town," the little Southern woman said in her familiar drawl, "and that Canada was a very relaxed country."

"It usually is," Arthur Kulas said. "I can't begin to explain what was behind the trouble last night. Perhaps the police will find out when they catch them."

"Let us hope they do," Colonel Hooper said with great dignity. "Such crimes should not go unpunished. Will you join us for cocktails at five, Mr. Kulas?"

The ex-diplomat bowed. "I'll be delighted to. It will be a pleasure to enjoy your company after all that has happened."

Carol worked with her employer repacking the three trunks. And for the first time she had a good chance to examine the exquisite materials he used in his lecture.

As they were finishing, Arthur Kulas came over to her, carrying a small rug of rich design in red, gold and green. "This has a special significance for me today," he told her, displaying the rug. "It happens to be the one Sousa gave me after he went to jail. It was my only contact with the fellow. Why they got the idea he gave me a map I can't imagine."

Carol studied the rug with admiring eyes. "It's very unusual," she said. "What does the design mean?"

Arthur Kulas furrowed his distinguished brow. "I honestly can't tell you except that it is typically Arabic. They have so many variations it is hard to keep track of them. I'm fond of the colors, aren't you? The yarn must have been dyed by a master."

"I agree," she said.

"Well, enough of that." Her employer sighed as he folded the rug up and packed it in the last open trunk. "Now we can have these trunks taken back to my room and locked in the closet."

Carol was glad the task was over and that she'd have a few minutes to enjoy the sunshine before having lunch and reporting to the hospital.

Word of the events at the old house on Chamcook Lake had spread around the hospital, and novelist Donald Winter, who was an ambulatory patient, stopped her in the corridor and asked her a host of questions about what had happened.

The popular writer was wearing vivid crimson pajamas and a dressing gown of rich gold brocade. "Sounds fantastic," he said. "Come to my room, and we'll build ourselves a story." He reached out for her in the Colonel Hooper manner.

She dodged a step back expertly and said with a grim smile, "I'm afraid the thing we'd build in your room would be mainly gossip, Mr. Winter. Please behave."

The novelist laughed. "You could be right. But wouldn't it be worth it?" And he moved on.

Mrs. Anderson was dressed and packing her suitcase when Carol went into her room. The wealthy woman at once came over and embraced the nurse warmly. "You poor child!" she exclaimed. "What an experience you must have gone through! Have the police caught those criminals yet?"

Carol smiled. "I'm afraid not."

The wealthy woman sighed. "I know the hotel management is frantic about it. Timothy Ryan phoned me and told me he's positively ill."

"I'm sure it will all quiet down," Carol said.

"And when it does we must have our party." Mrs. Anderson beamed. "And I won't forget to invite you. I promise."

"Let me help you finish your packing," Carol said. She stayed with the pleasant matron and carried her suitcase out to her car. Mrs. Anderson waved from the rear seat as her chauffeur drove her off.

When Carol went back into the hospital, she stopped by to see the stout Muriel Capper. The big woman looked downcast, even though a round clergyman was sitting in the room with her.

"This is Vicar Smith," Mrs. Capper introduced him. "He often plays the drums to my piano. But he isn't very good."

The rolypoly clergyman looked shocked. "Mrs. Capper! Whatever will this young lady think of me?"

"That you're not a very good musician," Muriel Capper said dryly. She leaned back on her pillows and addressed Carol. "So Mrs. Anderson has gone home?"

"Just now."

"I wish it was me," the stout woman mourned. "I don't know why the doctor keeps me in bed. I feel fine."

"It's necessary to be especially cautious in heart cases," Carol told the stout woman gently. "I'm sure the doctor is doing what he considers best for you."

Vicar Smith gave a nod, and his double chins quivered. "That's just what I've been telling her," he agreed.

Mildred Capper glared at him. "You're not only a poor musician you're a poor comforter," she said.

Carol left them to the argument which they were plainly enjoying.

Dr. Shaw was seated at his desk when she entered his office. He had an envelope and X-ray plates set out in front of him, and there was a look of despair and utter weariness on his pleasant face. The sandy-haired man waved to her to close the door after her.

"I've just gotten these plates," he said. "They came from the hospital in St. Stephen. They're pictures of the esophagus of one of the local businessmen who has done most to support my work here at the hospital." He made a disgusted gesture toward the plates with his hand. "The X-ray shows a tumor, terribly widespread and undoubtedly malignant. Too advanced for surgery to do any good."

Carol frowned. "Are you sure?"

He shrugged. "It's the verdict of the St. Stephen doctors. Take a look at the plates yourself."

She picked up the several plates and held them to the light of the window. Although she was not an expert at reading X-rays, the growth was obvious enough to her.

"It does look massive," she agreed solemnly.

"The man is fifty," Dr. Bill Shaw said. "How do I break the news of a thing like this to a friend?"

She turned to him again and placed the plates back on the desk top. Her expression was sympathetic. "But you must have been through this many times before."

He looked up at her. "I have," he agreed. "It never gets any easier. And this time it's someone close to me."

"I know how you must feel," she agreed. "Is he in the hospital?"

"No. He's at his home. They sent him there from the St. Stephen hospital. I'm supposed to stop by this afternoon." He got up, stuffed his hands in his pockets and moved toward the window with his head bent. "What can I say?"

"I'd tell him the truth: that it is very serious," she said. "He deserves that."

He glanced at her, his head still bent. "And then?"

"Suggest that he try an operation. It's his only hope, even in a case as advanced as this. And who knows, it may turn out to be less widespread than the X-ray plates show. They often are not completely accurate."

Dr. Bill Shaw looked up, and there was a sudden light of hope on his serious face. "I didn't think about that possibility," he said.

"You could be right." Then his face shadowed again. "But St. Stephen are dead against operating, and it is too big a case to handle here."

"Why not try Boston?" she suggested. "I know several surgeons in Boston who specialize in this type of case. I can even suggest a name. And you can talk it over with the patient. If he decides to go ahead, you can phone Boston and see if you can make arrangements for him."

The young doctor took a step toward her. "That's exactly what my procedure would be if the case hadn't been listed as hopeless in St. Stephen." He looked at her earnestly. "You think I should go ahead on that basis anyway?"

"I think your friend deserves a fighting chance," she said. "I know no other way of getting it."

Dr. Bill Shaw smiled. "You arrived at exactly the right moment, Carol. I was ready to give up."

"I wouldn't have expected that of you," she said quietly.

Bill Shaw's eyes continued to remain fixed on hers. He said, "I'm just beginning to realize how important you've become in my life."

Chapter Twelve

The next several weeks were placid. Things got back to normal at the resort hotel, and Carol continued her part-time work at the St. Andrews hospital. There were no more attacks or attempted robberies directed against Arthur Kulas, and he seemed to improve greatly in health. A great deal of his time was spent in the company of Colonel Hooper and his wife, who continued to stay on at the Mic-Mac Lodge, much to Captain Tim Mullaney's disgust.

At the hospital, Carol had been able to take part in a number of interesting minor operations and still was of the opinion that Dr. Bill Shaw was too good a surgeon to waste his talents as a general practitioner. And one morning in late August, when they were resting on the Casino steps after a game of tennis, she told him so.

"I think you should specialize in surgery," she informed the young man in tennis whites.

He smiled wryly and gazed down at the sidewalk. "I don't know. I'd like to. But sometimes I think it's too late. After all, I'm settled here. And I have built up a respectable practice."

"Which is leading no place in particular,"

she said. "You should try to find a younger man to take over and use your skill where it's needed most."

He gazed at her with a fond look. "Maybe I could do it with the right helpmate."

"You should have the determination to do it on your own," she insisted.

"I'll think about it," he said, staring across the lawn in the direction of the hotel swimming pool. And then he smiled at her. "I hate to say it, but this place has lost some of its glamour with the departure of Mimi Gamal. She was the queen of the pool!"

"She was a criminal!" Carol protested with a laugh.

"But an interesting one," the young doctor pointed out. "They haven't had any luck catching up with them, have they?"

"No," she said. "Mr. Kulas is furious. He thinks the police handled the case incompetently."

"I don't agree," Bill said. "I doubt if these people had any previous criminal records, at least not on this side of the Atlantic. They happened to know about that stolen treasure and were sure Sousa had given your boss a map showing where it was located. It would be the easiest thing in the world for them to scatter and vanish."

"That's apparently what they've managed

to do," she said.

He looked at his wristwatch. "Time to get back to my calls," he said.

"We had a good game," Carol told him as they both stood up. "Thanks."

"I'll be sorry when the summer ends," he told her. And then, changing the subject, he said. "By the way, I had word from Boston today about my friend with the cancer of the esophagus. The operation went well, and he seems to be making a good recovery."

"I'm glad to hear it," she said sincerely.

Dr. Shaw sighed. "Not that he's out of the woods. I doubt if he'll make a complete recovery. He may not get more than a few extra months. But at least there is a chance."

"I consider that the important thing," she agreed as they reached the sidewalk.

The young doctor again gazed across at the swimming pool, where a large group of the summer hotel guests were gathered. "I wouldn't mind having a dip right now instead of going back to work. I see your friend is there."

She lifted her eyebrows and turned to study the distant pool. "What friend?" she asked, peering to see who he meant."

"That Boston fellow, Walter Pitt," the doctor said. "What is he — some kind of millionaire? He has spent almost all summer here. Came here about the same time you and Mr. Kulas did."

Carol felt her cheeks burn as she spotted the young man from Boston poised on the pool's diving board. As he executed a perfect dive into the pool, she said, "I don't know too much about him. Of course he is staying at the Crest Hotel, and it's not nearly as expensive as the Mic-Mac."

"That's true," Bill Shaw admitted. "But their rates aren't that low. He must be pretty well fixed. Do you see much of him?"

Carol tried to play it cool as she shrugged. "Every now and then we meet. The Crest and the Mic-Mac have exchanged privileges for their guests, so he comes up here a lot."

"So I see," the young doctor observed dryly. "Well, I must be on my way. See you at the hospital this afternoon."

Carol waited until he drove away before walking back to the verandah of the resort hotel. She would have an hour or so before lunch. As she passed the pool, a dripping, bronzed Walter Pitt in black trunks waved to her.

Then he came running across the lawn to join her, his hair matted on his forehead and giving him a boyish appearance. "Hi!" he said in his usual enthusiastic way. "Did you have a good game with the old saw-bones?"

Carol glared at him. "That's not a proper way to speak of Dr. Shaw. And as for his being old, he can't be much more than your age."

"Don't believe it," Walter Pitt teased her. "I'm prematurely wrinkled. Too much responsibility and worry. You should feel sorry for me."

"I do," she said, "lazing away the whole summer. You should take a lesson from the doctor and do something useful with your life."

The young man from Boston assumed a solemn look. "I've been thinking that very thing," he said. "And with your help, I'll begin at the Casino dance tonight. I want to improve my cha-cha."

Carol shook her head. "You're impossible!" she said.

"I have a sense of humor," he called after her as she moved on. "That's more than the sawbones does."

Carol pretended not to hear him and kept on her way to the broad verandah of the resort hotel with its wicker chairs. She found one and sat down to enjoy the cool air and sunshine. She considered changing into her bathing suit and having a swim herself, but knew that would mean bumping into Walter Pitt again and so decided against it. The young man from Boston had a way of irritating her.

The old part of it was she also found him likable. It was a disturbing combination. Like Dr. Bill Shaw, she couldn't help wondering about his resources and how he could afford to spend the entire summer idling in the resort town. But he didn't impress her as being stupid or lazy. And now another thought came to her, one that had bothered her several times before, although she'd hastily put it to the back of her mind.

Suppose he was another of the crooks, trying to find out the secret of Sousa's buried treasure? It could be that he was biding his time and making friends with her and Arthur Kulas in order to have a showdown at the right moment. She hoped this wasn't the case, but she couldn't help remembering how friendly he'd been with the dusky-skinned Mimi Gamal.

She gazed out at the pool and saw that he was in the water, splashing around happily. It was hard to believe he could be involved in the plot against her employer. She didn't want to think about it. And anyhow, it was time to get ready for lunch. She rose hastily and went inside.

That afternoon there was a minor crisis at the hospital. One of the elderly patrons of the Mic-Mac Lodge was rushed there by car. He was a stout man in his late sixties and was gasping for breath when he was helped into the examination room.

"When did you first feel ill?" Bill Shaw asked the man.

"After I left the golf course this morning," the stout vacationer managed in choked tones.

Meanwhile Bill was checking him as Carol helped. The young doctor asked, "Have you been nauseated?"

The stout man nodded miserably. "Yes, Doctor. I tried to eat lunch and lost it. I'm dizzy and my heart is beating too fast, and my neck feels tight, as if I were going to suffocate."

The young doctor gave him a reassuring smile. "Nothing like that is likely to happen to you. We're going to put you in bed for some rest, and you'll be all right. You've been overdoing it."

When the patient was being prepared for bed in a private room by one of the orderlies and Nurse Caine, Bill told Carol, "This man had a mild heart attack. But we won't tell him that. No need to scare him."

She nodded. "The symptoms seemed familiar."

"Irritable focus in the ventricles," he said. "The ventricular beat is almost a hundred and seventy a minute. He'll need close watching. My guess is he's had organic heart disease and hasn't known it."

"It probably hasn't shown up this way before," she suggested.

Bill looked grim. "Sometimes these people vacation harder than they work. He'll need extended bed rest and drug therapy. No digitalis. I'd suggest quinidine orally every two or three hours. I'll make out an order for it."

So Carol devoted most of her time until she left to the unhappy stout man. Because of his nausea, the drug had to be injected, and when she went at six he was still in an uneasy state. She felt somewhat guilty at leaving the tense atmosphere of the hospital to return to the leisurely life of the hotel.

Arthur Kulas was in his best mood at dinner. He was wearing one of his expensive, finely tailored English suits and looking dignified. As the orchestra offered dinner music in the background, he confided to Carol, "The social life is coming to a peak as the season ends. The hotel will be closing in a week, you know."

"I've been so busy I hadn't thought about it," Carol admitted.

The distinguished, gray-haired man smiled at her. "Well, you'd better begin to think about it. We'll be leaving for Boston a week from Sunday, so you'd better give that young doctor notice you'll no longer be available for work at the hospital after that."

"I will," she said, feeling somewhat dismayed. The hospital had become a part of her daily existence.

"I shall be glad to return to Boston," Arthur Kulas went on. "It will be good to be back in my apartment again. And thanks to you, I'm feeling much better. As you know, my insulin intake has greatly decreased."

She smiled. "I'd say the air and sunshine here have helped. And the rest."

"It's been a good vacation," he admitted, "except for that one unhappy incident. And I'm sure Timothy Ryan could have prevented that."

Carol made no comment. She couldn't conceive how the chubby assistant manager could be blamed for the attack Mimi Gamal and her cohorts had made on them. But it was typical of her employer that he blamed the little man.

"Tomorrow morning the colonel and his

wife have invited us for a sail," her employer went on happily. "You know I've never been out in the *Cynthia,* and they're planning to leave in a few days."

"That will be nice," she said vaguely.

"And they want you to come along."

Carol became mildly upset. "I don't see how I can," she said. "I have to report at the hospital at one."

"You can miss tennis for one morning," her employer said. "And I'll ask Dr. Shaw to allow you to report to the hospital late, if necessary."

"They're so rushed I'd rather not," she protested.

"Nonsense!" Arthur Kulas said in his most stubborn tone. "After all, your main duty is to me. I have priority, as your employer and private patient. And if it is fine tomorrow, I insist you go along on the boat."

Carol privately hoped the fog would come in or it would rain. But there had been little fog or rain at St. Andrews all season, and the next day was sunny and warm. She knew there would be no avoiding the trip on the *Cynthia.*

Arthur Kulas was in a jubilant mood as they drove down to the wharf. And she tried to respond, not wanting to spoil his day. But when she saw Walter Pitt standing on

200

the wharf in faded slacks and an open-necked shirt, she was ready to turn back and head for the hotel.

"Are you going along?" she asked in astonishment.

"I really wasn't invited," he admitted.

"I know," she said dismally. "You crashed the party!"

"I hate to admit it, but I did." He smiled happily. "At least I'll have you along to keep me company."

"Don't count on it," she warned him, certain her day was going to be a disaster.

At least there was one consolation. Neither Captain Tim Mullaney nor their hosts, Colonel and Ellen Hooper, seemed pleased that the young man was forcing his company on them. He was given cold looks as he bounced aboard after Carol stepped onto the deck of the big yacht. Within a few minutes, Captain Tim Mullaney cast off, and they were heading out on the silver waters of the bay.

The bearded Irishman came to stand by Carol in the bow. "I'm glad we're making this trip," he told her. "It will give you a sample of my seamanship."

She smiled at him. "I'm sure you're very competent."

"A man like me is lost on land," he said,

gazing out at the sun-swept waters. "This is my domain."

In the bow of the luxurious craft, Colonel Hooper and Ellen were hosting a delighted Arthur Kulas at a cocktail party. The colonel's hooting laughter mingled with Ellen's gentle cooing and the pleased chuckles of the ex-diplomat.

Captain Tim Mullaney gazed toward the rear of the *Cynthia*. "I guess they are having a good time," he said.

"I'm sure of it," Carol responded. She stared at the coastline fading away. "It's exciting. I'm glad I came."

"We'll be out of sight of land before we turn back," the captain predicted. "The *Cynthia* has good speed." And he glanced at the upper deck where Walter Pitt was standing by himself, staring around. "We have one uninvited guest," he said in a disgusted tone.

"I know," she agreed. "He does like to crash parties. But I'm sure he means no harm."

The red-bearded man stared up at him grimly. "I haven't much liking for the playboy type," he said. And with a tip of his nautical cap: "If you'll excuse me a minute, I have some sea duties."

Carol wasn't left long. A moment later the

young man from Boston had come down to stand beside her. "Having fun?" he asked.

She gave him a cool look. "Yes," she said. "I was invited."

"I wasn't, and I'm enjoying it just the same," he told her happily.

She stared at him in concern. "Walter Pitt, what is wrong with you? You don't seem to have any self-respect! You laze around this summer resort week after week and crash every party! You're a kind of parasite!"

The young man from Boston looked hurt. "But I'm an agreeable parasite," he insisted.

"I know that," she said. "I almost let myself like you. But today is the last straw. You had no right coming on this boat without being properly invited. And you shouldn't be wasting your time in a summer resort anyway. You should be working!"

"Bravo, Miss Holly, that's telling him!" It was Captain Tim Mullaney who encouraged her in his Irish brogue. She turned to look his way and found herself staring into the cold muzzle of a gun. She gave a gasp of surprise and fear.

Walter Pitt's tanned face also showed astonishment. "What sort of game it this?" he demanded.

The red-bearded captain covered them with the gun. "I don't care what you call it," he said. "You asked for it by insisting on coming aboard. Now I'll get you to move down to the bow and join the eminent Mr. Kulas."

Carol and the young man from Boston exchanged troubled glances and then did as he said. They had some difficulty keeping their footing, as the boat was in rough water and heaving a good deal. When they joined Arthur Kulas, he was seated in a deck chair, looking ill. Colonel Hooper was standing before him like an angry questioning eagle, and the demure Ellen, looking a good deal less like a Southern lady than usual, was covering Kulas with a tiny revolver.

Colonel Hooper glared at them with his shrewd blue eyes as they approached. He waved toward a couple of empty deck chairs beside Arthur Kulas. "Sit down there" he rasped, "the two of you!"

Arthur Kulas looked at them weakly. "I don't know," he murmured as if the end of the world had arrived.

As they seated themselves, Carol in the middle chair, Ellen Hooper's tiny red face showed anger. "But you do know, Mr. Kulas. We have definite information Sousa gave you that map. And we want it!"

"She's right!" Colonel Hooper said, jabbing a finger at the astonished ex-diplomat.

"Sousa claims you always keep the map with you, that it is never far away from you. So hand it over, or you'll not see land again!"

The unhappy Kulas groaned. "But I tell you I don't know anything about a map. The scoundrel has been lying as usual."

Colonel Hooper shook his bald head. "Sousa had his throat slit in prison before he told the truth. He did not lie about it."

"So you'd better talk, and fast, Mr. Kulas," the diminutive Ellen snarled, "before we toss you and your friends into the Bay of Fundy."

Kulas stared at them incredulously. "How could you do this? I regarded you as my friends, wonderful people!"

"Don't worry about that," Colonel Hooper snapped. "What about the map?"

The diplomat swallowed hard. "You can do what you like," he said. "I don't know anything about it, and I'm telling you the truth when I say that."

The red-bearded Captain Mullaney's expression was anything but genial now. He gave the colonel an ugly glance. "Maybe a little pressure used in the right way will help Mr. Kulas talk. You just lost a tooth or two last time," he told the diplomat. "This time we could be a little rougher."

"Hold it!" It was Walter Pitt who spoke

up, and there was a barely concealed note of triumph in his tone. "I think all of you would be wise to go easy. We have company."

Their startled captors turned simultaneously to see a fast power boat bearing down on them. Captain Tim Mullaney uttered an angry oath. The colonel and his wife appeared crestfallen. The little woman let the hand with the gun in it drop limply.

"If I'm not mistaken," Walter Pitt went on, "that is the Mounted Police patrol boat. And it appears they're going to hail us for a routine inspection. They take fine care of the vessels in these waters."

Of course his ridiculous luck held good. The Mounted Police boat did come alongside for a routine check, and Arthur Kulas at once told the police of their predicament. Colonel Hooper and his wife protested their innocence, as did the captain. But the police were not that easily convinced and escorted the *Cynthia* back to port, where the three were taken in custody pending further investigation of the matter.

Fingerprints from Washington proved the colonel to be an international crook and Ellen his accomplice. Captain Mullaney also had a criminal record and was wanted by the police in Baltimore.

Arthur Kulas was completely disillusioned. He couldn't get away from the hotel and return to Boston quickly enough. Walter Pitt vanished finally, and Carol assumed he had gone back to Boston and his career as a writer. She felt he'd experienced enough adventures during the exciting summer to write about. And she couldn't help wishing he'd taken the time to say goodbye to her before he left.

The time had come to bid farewell to the St. Andrews hospital and Dr. Bill Shaw. The young man received the news of her departure disconsolately as she told him in his office.

He got up and came from behind the desk. "I'd hoped you might decide to stay here," he said.

She shook her head with a sad smile. "No. I don't think this is the place for either of us. I'm positive you should go somewhere else and specialize."

"I'm thinking about it," he said.

"Let me know when you decide," she told him gently.

Their eyes met, and he took her hands in his. "I'll miss you, Carol," he said in a husky voice. "It's been great." And he drew her close to him and touched his lips to her forehead.

What might have happened next was

impossible to predict, for at that moment the stout Nurse Cain burst into the office saying, "I'm sorry, Doctor, but we have an emergency — a man with a badly cut hand."

Bill Shaw gave Carol a sad smile. "You see how it is," he said, and quickly left her.

She didn't see him again. The drive back to Boston was pleasant, and Arthur Kulas appeared to regain his good spirits along the way. He enjoyed the scenery and relaxed.

"At least that should mark the end of the robbery attempts," he said. "I can look forward to some peace in Boston."

"Aren't Mimi Gamal and Westy still at large?" she asked.

The diplomat hunched down in his seat. "I wish you hadn't reminded me of that," he said with a frown.

When they reached his Beacon Street apartment she saw him safely inside and informed him it was her opinion he no longer required her services. Considering that he was a good deal of a neurotic, the ex-diplomat accepted the ultimatum very well.

"I agree, Miss Holly," he said amiably. "But I do want our association to end on a pleasant note. I'd like you to join me for dinner tomorrow night. I'll have it sent in by the catering firm who looks after my simple needs."

Carol glanced around the elegant living room of the apartment. It would be hard to leave the luxurious surroundings and life she'd enjoyed for the past few months and go back to her bleak boarding-house room and regular private duty. The invitation was too good to refuse.

She smiled at the handsome older man. "I'll be glad to come," she said.

His eyes gleamed with delight. "Wear something especially smart," he told her. "We'll make it a gala affair."

And so the next evening, at seven sharp, she returned to the apartment, wearing a yellow dress with shimmering sequins on it. She'd taken the day off to rest and have her hair done in an updo so she'd look her best.

Arthur Kulas received her with an admiring smile. "Exquisite," he said. "I approve of everything. And I have the proper corsage waiting for you: a white orchid."

"Thank you," she said. "You've gone to so much trouble!"

"Don't thank me for the orchid," he told her with a glint in his eyes. "It was a friend's idea and gift. There will be three of us for dinner."

Carol was curious. And a few minutes

later, when the bell rang and her host went to answer it, she began to feel nervous. Who would it be? Was it someone she'd feel at ease with?

And then her former employer returned with a smiling Walter Pitt at his side. Arthur Kulas said, "The third guest. Of course you know Miss Holly."

The young man from Boston, looking handsome in a dinner jacket, smiled. "To be truthful, this is the first time we've been properly introduced."

Carol gasped. "You again!"

He nodded. "I've crashed another party."

Arthur Kulas had his arm around the young man's shoulders. "That's not true at all. I invited him. May I explain? Walter is a private detective who has been taking care of my welfare all summer."

"And not too well, I'm afraid," the young man from Boston said.

"I won't complain this time," the distinguished ex-diplomat said. "He's just brought me word they've rounded up Mimi, Westy and the other two. So it's over. And most importantly, we know about the map."

Carol was too astonished to take it all in properly. "The map?" she echoed.

"The one they all wanted so badly," Arthur Kulas said. "It was woven into the back of the rug. Of course I'd never have dreamed it if Walter hadn't figured it out." He gave the young man an admiring look. "Clever boy! So now the rug is on its way back to the proper government authorities, who can seek out the stolen treasure. And I can go back to holding my lectures without interference."

"I certainly hope so," Walter Pitt said.

The ex-diplomat glanced at the candle-lit table and then at his wristwatch. "Dear me! The caterers are late with the food as usual. If you two will excuse me a moment, I'll just give them a ring." And he smiled brightly and went out, leaving them together in the softly lighted room.

Carol got up. "I know him. And he doesn't look upset. It's a conspiracy between you two. He used that as an excuse to leave you here alone with me."

The young man from Boston went over to her with a smile. "You know, that's an excellent bit of deduction," he said. "I think you'd make a first-rate detective, or at least a wonderful detective's wife." And he took her in his arms for a lasting kiss.

As far as Carol was concerned, she wasn't in a mood to dispute him. She was too busy responding!

We hope you have enjoyed this Large Print book. Other Thorndike, Wheeler, and Chivers Press Large Print books are available at your library or directly from the publishers.

For information about current and upcoming titles, please call or write, without obligation, to:

Publisher
Thorndike Press
295 Kennedy Memorial Drive
Waterville, ME 04901
Tel. (800) 223-1244

or visit our Web site at:

www.gale.com/thorndike
www.gale.com/wheeler

OR

Chivers Large Print
published by BBC Audiobooks Ltd
St James House, The Square
Lower Bristol Road
Bath BA2 3SB
England
Tel. +44(0) 800 136919
email: bbcaudiobooks@bbc.co.uk
www.bbcaudiobooks.co.uk

All our Large Print titles are designed for easy reading, and all our books are made to last.